Paul Wenz was born in 1869 int
family. He first visited Australia
in New South Wales in 1898. He
Dunne, and took up a large proper
Forbes and Cowra. Before the First World he published a number
of short stories written in French and set mostly in Australia;
in 1908 his only work written in English, *Diary of a New Chum*,
was published in Melbourne. He visited Europe regularly and
served as a liaison officer in France during the war. From 1919
to 1931 he published four novels, some memoirs and more short
stories, all of which were published in Paris. He became more
involved in Australian literary life during this period, but because
he wrote in French he remained unknown to all but a few until
his death in Forbes in 1939.

Maurice Blackman is a senior lecturer in French at the university
of New South Wales. He is also director of the French-Australian
Research Centre at the university, where he is actively involved
in researching French-Australian connections. Dr Blackman has
also published in the area of modern French literature.

into a wealthy French wool-buying
in 1892 and decided to settle
married an Australian, Harriet
on the Lachlan River between

IMPRINT

DIARY OF A NEW CHUM
and Other Lost Stories

PAUL WENZ

Preface by Frank Moorhouse
Edited and translated by Maurice Blackman
with translations by Patricia Brulant and Margaret Whitlam
and notes by Jean-Paul Delamotte

ANGUS
& ROBERTSON

Collins/Angus & Robertson Publishers'
creative writing programme
is assisted by the
Australia Council, the
Australian Government's
arts advisory and
support organisation.

Arts for
Australians
Australia **Council**

AN ANGUS & ROBERTSON BOOK

First published in Australia in 1990 by
Collins/Angus & Robertson Publishers Australia

Collins/Angus & Robertson Publishers Australia
Unit 4, Eden Park, 31 Waterloo Road, North Ryde
NSW 2113, Australia

William Collins Publishers Ltd
31 View Road, Glenfield, Auckland 10, New Zealand

Angus & Robertson (UK)
16 Golden Square, London W1R 4BN, United Kingdom

National Library of Australia
Cataloguing-in-Publication data:

Wenz, Paul.
  Diary of a new chum and other lost stories.
  ISBN 0 207 16673 0.
  I. Title.
A823.2

Typeset in 11/12 pt Times Roman by Midland Typesetters
Printed in Australia by Globe Press

Cover photograph: Paul Wenz (left) with Jack London, in Sydney. (courtesy Mitchell Library)

5 4 3 2 1
95 94 93 92 91 90

CONTENTS

Reading Paul Wenz by Frank Moorhouse   1

A French-Australian Writer by Maurice Blackman   5

DIARY OF A NEW CHUM   17

SELECTED STORIES   53

How Bill Larkins Went to the Paris Exhibition   55

Charley   67

Jim and Jack   73

Picky   78

His Dog   90

Fifty-five Minutes Late   93

The Spoonbill Hut   97

The Waggoner   112

UNPUBLISHED TEXTS   127

The Gazelle   129

Lone Joe   134

Jack London   141

SELECTED LETTERS   143

Correspondence with André Gide   145

Australian Correspondence   166

Biographical Outline   176

Acknowledgements   198

READING PAUL WENZ

by Frank Moorhouse

Don't anticipate that you will find a lost genius in the writings of Paul Wenz. Paul Wenz was a good writer, not a great writer, by the literary criteria of today. But Wenz's stories such as 'The Waggoner' should be in our standard anthologies.

What Maurice Blackman and Jean-Paul Delamotte have done is to use the work of Paul Wenz to create an enchanting book greater than Paul Wenz's stories. It is a literary collage which celebrates Paul Wenz's presence in Australia and reapproaches the storytelling which Wenz left us.

As the core of the book there are the stories of Paul Wenz which have accreted interest with the passing of time and because of his exceptional place in our literary history. The stories have not been widely known—they were 'lost' to us temporarily. A young culture can savour some things which an older and more elaborate culture might pass over. We have to savour what we have. Wenz was even rarer for a young culture—a person from a sophisticated literary culture (and personal background) living in and writing about the new culture—not as a professional observer but as someone who was working in the culture, integrated into it.

I say that the work of Wenz has accreted interest. By that I mean that it has more to say to us than its literary intention. The stories' resonances work above and beyond the service given by the narrative.

Importantly, Maurice Blackman and Jean-Paul Delamotte have written their notes and commentary which become components of the Wenz collage. To this are added the letters of Wenz to Nobel prize-winner-to-be André Gide and Wenz's letters to and from Australian writers. In their own context these letters could be considered unremarkable but given the context

1

of this literary collage, they come to life in another way.

The book is rich in curious details of social history. In the shapely account of Wenz's meeting with Jack London in Sydney in 1909, Wenz gives a sharp, quick portrait of the writer as Visiting Celebrity and as an aside, we learn about coffee drinking in Australia. In another story Wenz notes that a woman on board a P&O ship to France in first class ate formidable amounts of salt with her food and that the menu was in French but the cuisine was English. I like these details.

There is Christopher Brennan's letter to Wenz where Brennan wriggles out of giving a gift copy of his poems and instead bills Wenz for the price of a volume, charging extra for the archival value of his signature and post-publication corrections.

There are the personal resonances which any nice work of literature gives us. I saw that Paul Wenz used the pen name 'Warrego'. For a few years in my twenties I wore Warrego shirts bought from Peepes, the gentlemen's outfitter in George Street, Sydney, a classic Australian shirt similar to the R. M. Williams' Bush Shirt—flap pockets, half buttoned down the front and as the assistant at Peepes once said to me, 'Room enough in the shoulders, sir, to swing an axe!'

Anyone who has lost their wallet (or American Express card) will empathise with the story of Bill Larkins when he is pickpocketed in Port Said. And weep.

There is the observation in 'The Jackaroo' of the special depression which comes on people who work alone in the bush— a neurosis caused by the deprivation of human society. A few of his studies are of the psychopathology of bush life with the ache of sexual frustration, the clumsy protocols of bush courtship and of the pain of the men frightened of women. There is the story of the emotionally wounded young man who could not drink in a bar where a woman was serving.

This bush neurosis is further explored in the 'Lone Joe' who in his isolation and in the illusion of self-sufficiency becomes infatuated with a goanna.

The neurosis was solaced by a dependence on alcohol and

tobacco. 'A pipe is a companion in the bush, its bowl is full of dreams. We watch the smoke rising . . . around which sad thoughts swirl heavily like thick mists.'

There is the curious detail in a letter to Wenz from André Gide where Gide implies that he has studied a photograph of a steam-driven plough with sixteen ploughshares sent by Wenz and has counted the ploughshares and can find only fifteen. Wenz explains in another letter that one of the ploughshares is out of the picture.

There is a description of an early rabbit-poisoning machine.

There is the observation of the importance of verandahs in country towns—one verandah-post for every man in the town to lean on.

In the stories there is a record of a passing ethos. It is 1910 and Jessie is five years old. She can already mount a horse by herself and bring in the cows. 'She helped her mother with the household chores as best she could, and like any self-respecting Australian kid, she could already set to work with an American axe on anything that an axe can chop.'

I am interested in the romantic revival of lost bushcrafts and I am always pleased to find that the people who had to live by these crafts were not necessarily so pleased with them at the time. In books of bushcraft I have come across the celebrated slush lamp made from animal fats. Wenz describes it in 1908. 'A slush lamp is a contrivance which smokes and smells a lot, but gives little light. It was invented during the Stone Age, and has never been improved since.'

Wenz records 'bush types' such as the mechanically talented bush carpenter who can fix anything. He is asked if he could make a piano. The bush carpenter says, 'Maybe I could . . . only them notes would be the trouble . . .'

Even though Wenz was from another culture he seems to have been inescapably enfolded in the Australian bush mythology. His stories and characters are so familiar because they are fully within the conventions of the bush story. It showed me how strong the conventions were—how they determined what literature could 'see' and what was not seen, the boundaries of perception. I have an ongoing debate with myself about whether this way of seeing the bush in literature was mythological—a narrative imposed on an indistinct, slippery reality by a community urgently trying to find an acceptable definition of itself—or whether it was also the 'way things really were' or how much of it is the way things really were. I think the Wenz stories are further evidence of the way Australia wanted to see itself—a use of narrative to create a consoling equilibrium of shared pain—one of the services storytelling does for society.

Regardless of the search for historically valid description, and regardless of this theoretical reading of Wenz, his work can still be enjoyed as wonderful storytelling.

In his list of advice to new chums about dealing with Australians, Wenz says, 'Don't try to make them believe that we, too, have sunsets in Europe.'

Wenz, like all good observers from another culture, reminded me, not always intentionally, that we *do* have remarkable sunsets in the Australian bush, but more than that—that people in the bush once thought this rather special, that they lived a life of few diversions and that the setting of the sun and the cool respite which comes with it in the bush was something to be appreciated with daily wonder.

We have to thank Jean-Paul Delamotte for giving Paul Wenz back to us. This book is a vibrant part of our national memory and, like all good history, the book 're-minds' us and re-makes that memory.

4

A FRENCH-AUSTRALIAN WRITER:

by Maurice Blackman

Who was Paul Wenz?

He was born in 1869 into a wealthy French Protestant family; his father had originally come from Wurtemberg in Germany, and he owned woollen mills in Rheims. The family company imported wool from South America and Australia. At the age of ten he was sent off to a fairly exclusive private school in Paris, where he seems to have had an average career, although he was reportedly good at written composition; one of his schoolmates was André Gide. After leaving school and performing his compulsory military service, Wenz had a brief initiation into the family business, decided he didn't really like being cooped up in an office, and was sent off to London for the best part of a year to learn English, and presumably to find out more about the wool-importing trade.

Wenz's eldest brother had travelled in Australia and New Zealand in 1884, and as a result of his visit the wool-broking agency Wenz and Co had been established with branches in Sydney and Melbourne. (The agency was quickly successful, and remained a force in the wool trade until the 1970s.)

Paul Wenz was an active, outgoing young man who had a hearty appetite for travel and the outdoor life—it was an appetite that he would maintain until the end of his days. At the end of 1890 he set off to Algeria to try his hand at winegrowing; he encountered many difficulties, fell ill, and returned to France after about a year. In 1892 he arrived in Australia for the first time. He seems to have liked the country immediately, and he spent the next two years jackarooing in Victoria and NSW. He returned briefly to France at the end of 1894 but came back to the Pacific the following year, spending some time in New Caledonia and then in North Queensland. In 1896 he spent a few months in New Zealand, and then returned to France via Paraguay and Argentina.

Back in France he immediately made arrangements to emigrate to Australia, and on the ship coming out he met a young Australian woman, Harriet Dunne, a squatter's daughter; they became engaged soon after arrival. In 1898 he purchased, with the help of his family, a large sheep and cattle station on the Lachlan between Forbes and Cowra, and he and Harriet were married. He set himself up as a grazier in one of the prime districts of NSW and divided his time between running his property, Nanima, and overseeing the family's wool-broking agency, both of which were quite successful.

Wenz began his literary career in 1900, when the first of a series of short stories, written in French but set mostly in Australia, appeared in the Paris magazine *L'Illustration* under the pseudonym 'Paul Warrego'. These stories appeared over a number of years and mainly had Australian bush settings, although some were also set on South Pacific islands. Wenz and his wife returned to France for a long visit in 1905, and in that same year he published his first book, *A l'autre bout du monde* [At the Other End of the World]; this was a collection of stories, including some already published in *L'Illustration*, and it must have had some success, since it ran to a second edition in 1907. In 1908 he published in Melbourne his only book to be written in English, *Diary of a New Chum*.

At the end of 1908, the Wenzes met and became good friends with the American author Jack London and his wife Charmian, who were then visiting Sydney. Doubtless as a result of this friendship, Wenz undertook to translate into French one of London's books.

Wenz and his wife set off for France again in 1909, this time travelling through South-East Asia and China, thence by Trans-Siberian Railway to Europe. During their long stay in Europe, Wenz renewed contact with many old acquaintances, including André Gide, who by now was an author of some note and closely involved with the newly founded *Nouvelle Revue Française*. Gide was impressed with his old schoolfriend's doings and arranged for one of his stories to appear in the *NRF*. The Wenzes returned to Australia in 1910, and that same year there appeared a second collection of stories, *Sous la Croix du Sud* [Beneath the Southern Cross], this time published under Wenz's own name; again, they mostly have bush settings, with a few set on Pacific islands, and once more the stories ran to a second edition in 1911.

During his visit, Wenz had introduced Gide to the work of Jack London. In 1912 he sent the completed manuscript of his translation of *Love of Life* to Gide, and the *NRF* later published the work with great success in its literary collection. (Wenz's translation of this work is still currently available.)

After more travels and another long stay in France, Wenz and his wife were caught in Rheims at the outbreak of war in 1914: they decided to stay on in France and work for the Red Cross. In 1915 Wenz's first novel, *L'Homme du soleil couchant* [The Sundowner], which had been started before he left Australia, appeared in serial form in the *Revue de Paris*. From 1916 to 1918, with Australian troops now posted to the European front, Wenz was sent to London as a liaison officer with the Red Cross. During his time in England, Wenz had contacts, probably through Gide, with several writers, including Joseph Conrad, John Galsworthy and Arnold Bennett, and he wrote a second novel, *Le Pays de leurs pères* [Land of Their Fathers], which was also serialised in the *Revue de Paris*. Back in France in 1919, Wenz published two small collections of wartime stories set in France and England. In the same year *Le Pays de leurs pères* appeared as a book; although it was in fact his second novel, it was the first to be published in book form.

The Wenzes returned to Australia in August 1919 after an absence of more than six years, and Wenz seems to have resumed his life as a grazier with some gusto, apparently putting aside writing for the time being. A few stories, with English or French settings, appeared in the *Revue de Paris* and the *Revue Française* at the beginning of the 1920s, but they had most likely been written while Wenz was still in Europe; *L'Homme du soleil couchant* was published as a book in 1923, but that had been written nearly ten years before. Apart from a small book about his experiences as a sheep farmer, which appeared in 1925, Wenz published nothing more until the end of the decade. In 1929, 1930 and 1931, however, three books appeared in succession: *Le Jardin des Coraux* [The Coral Garden], a novel set in Sydney and on the Barrier Reef, *Il était une fois un gosse* [There Was Once a Silly Kid], a book of fanciful childhood memoirs, and *L'Echarde* [The Thorn in the Flesh], a novel set in South Australia. Also dating from the early 1930s are a number of mostly unpublished manuscripts—a book of travel memoirs, a group of *Arabian Nights*-style tales, another group of light-hearted stories for children (written for the children of his nieces and nephews in France: he had no children of his own), and a few more Australian bush stories.

Wenz's last publications during his lifetime were a story (in English) in the *Bulletin* in 1934 and an Arabian fable (in French) in *L'Illustration* in 1935; in 1937 he wrote another Australian bush novel but it was never published. After a final trip to England and France in 1938-39, he returned to Nanima and died in Forbes Hospital after a short illness in August 1939.

Wenz's literary career seems to have been that of a successful amateur writer. He remained virtually unknown in Australia because of the language he chose to write in, and he had a minor success in France with his pre-war stories, no doubt because of their exotic locations. He is a good storyteller with the right mix of wry humour and sentiment, and he is the first, and so far the only, writer to give the French reader a true picture of Australian bush life. His stories bespeak an ambiguous feeling towards the outback, and he always seems to maintain an ironic distance from his characters. He is good at descriptions, and is able to evoke the spell of the bush, its strange beauty but also its grim harshness. His Pacific island stories, much smaller in number, tend to deal in the clichés of the genre, but he always avoids painting an idealized picture of island life.

In his bush stories he usually adopts the point of view of a bemused new chum poking gentle fun at the ways of the bush types. His stories are peopled with character sketches of swaggies, boundary riders, solitary miners, bush publicans, shearers and rural workers, station bosses and storekeepers, and the stories range from the lightly humorous to the poignant, to the starkly horrific. The central character in both *Diary of a New Chum* and *L'Homme du soleil couchant* is an upper-class refugee new chum from England fleeing an unhappy or unwise love affair and although the latter work is an attempt to move towards the novel, it remains a series of sketches loosely threaded together. Most of the chapters could stand alone as short stories. Indeed, that was where Wenz's real talent lay; he seems never to have felt entirely at home in his novels. *Le Pays de leurs pères* shows a similar unease with the more sustained form, even if it is more tightly organised. A good part of the novel recounts the experiences of some Australian soldiers on leave and recuperating in England, and Wenz reverses his earlier device to portray their bemused reactions to the English and their way of life.

The later novels are more ambitious, with an interesting gothic flavour. *Le Jardin des Coraux* begins in an urban setting and follows its young Sydney couple as they go off for an idyllic honeymoon on an isolated coral island; the idyll turns to terror and then tragedy as an escaped criminal arrives on their island. Tension mounts until the husband is killed in a struggle; the wife is then terrorised until she manages to catch the criminal off guard and shoot him, after which she is forced to stay on the island with the two dead men until the supply boat comes. *L'Echarde* is a rather grim psychological study of the obsessive jealousy of a woman in love with a man she cannot have. She spends her life trying to make his life a misery until she herself is killed in a bitterly ironic twist of fate. A tale of unusual passion, *L'Echarde* has a more powerful and dramatic structure and is perhaps the most remarkable of his novels. His last unpublished

9

novel *Walkaringa* marks a return to the episodic saga form of *L'Homme du soleil couchant*, with its series of amusing and poignant sketches of life in an isolated outback community, and its contrived and rather too touching ending. Compared to *L'Echarde* or *Le Jardin des Coraux*, it is a feeble regression to earlier modes of writing, and it is not hard to see why it remained unpublished.

Now that I have sketched in the biographical background, we come to the difficult question of deciding whether Wenz is a French or an Australian writer. On the surface the case seems to be straightforward enough. Although his books deal mainly with Australia, and although he spent half his life here, Wenz always remained a French citizen, made regular long visits to his native country, was attached to the French Army during the war, wrote virtually all his work in French, and published it in France for French readers. One can understand why the Fisher Library catalogue feels it necessary to note on its cards that Wenz is a French writer, but is classified with Australian literature 'because of his local interest.'

On a deeper level, it is certainly clear that Wenz identified with the French literary scene: he read widely and regularly in contemporary French literature and maintained a library of the great writers; he kept up a correspondence with André Gide during his life in Australia, often discussing literary matters; and he maintained other literary contacts on his regular visits to France. In a number of respects, his writing is identifiably French, as we would expect. The most obvious French influence is Guy de Maupassant, and through him, the whole 'naturalist' movement in late nineteenth-century French writing. There are distinct affinities in both style and form between Maupassant's stories and those of Wenz, particularly in his pre-war short stories: their concise clear-cut form; the clarity and austerity of their style; their pervading irony, though it is gentler and more sympathetic than Maupassant's. Wenz has Maupassant's talent for the deft sketching of memorable character types, but he completely lacks Maupassant's cynicism, being of a more optimistic and sentimental disposition.

Wenz's more ambitious novels suggest traces of Gide, though without his metaphysical complexity. He shares with Gide an interest in the study of atypical or extreme psychological cases and a fascination with the ironies of fate amounting almost to a taste for the Absurd. A recurrent theme in Wenz as in Gide is the struggle between fragile civilisation and amoral nature, though Wenz is more preoccupied with the practical rather than the metaphysical aspects of such a theme. The austere clarity of the style, as well as the occasional appearance of melodramatic or gothic touches, also recall Gide.

Wenz himself would probably have been more conscious of internationalist or cosmopolitan influences. In his pre-war period he greatly admired, and occasionally imitated or translated, what might be called the 'virile' writers of hearty adventure and seafaring tales: Jack London, Joseph Conrad, R. L. Stevenson, our own Louis Becke, and minor writers like Morley Roberts. By 1920 he had also come to admire the 'social' writers like Wells, Bennett and Galsworthy, and tried his hand in that vein in a small number of mostly unpublished stories.

Particularly in the period before and during World War I, Wenz seems to have felt he was the interpreter and apologist for Australia and the Australian way of life to the French public. But what is perhaps more interesting for us is that in both style and subject matter he can be located within the Australian literary discourse at one of its key moments, precisely when that discourse was reflecting on its own identity.

Alongside the French and international influences in Wenz's writing, it is, if anything, easier to detect the Australian influences. Wenz the horseman and sheep-farmer personally appreciated the poetry of Adam Lindsay Gordon and the bush balladists, like the rest of his class, and was a regular reader of the *Bulletin*. As a writer, he knew well and greatly admired the stories of Henry Lawson, and recommended him to Gide; his own bush stories show that he was certainly influenced by the new *Bulletin* school of writing that was at its peak in the period 1890–1905.

Lawson's influence is everywhere apparent in the tone and

11

the subject matter of the bush stories: the frequent doses of pathos, sometimes lapsing into sentimentality; the good-natured ironic humour; the sympathy for the bush characters. It perhaps also extends to the frequently documentary quality of Wenz's writing, with its sharpness and selection of detail. However, Wenz is far less ambiguous in his attitude towards outback life, even if he shares Lawson's sense of awe at its harshness; in Wenz, this motif of the harshness of the bush usually serves to set off the understated, everyday heroism of his characters.

There are a few of Wenz's stories, it is true, which do explore a much more bleak and cruel aspect of the bush in ways which recall the grim horror and starkness of Barbara Baynton's bush world. Nevertheless, the prevailing atmosphere in Wenz's bush world usually recalls that of Steele Rudd's stories, and Wenz is much more at home with his style of disingenuous humour and his mixture of farce and seriousness. Finally, it is possible that the wry irony and apparently shapeless structure of Joseph Furphy's *Such is Life* find some echoes in Wenz's first essay at the novel, *L'Homme du soleil couchant*.

It is clear that in his pre-war writing, Wenz embraces wholeheartedly the collective attitude of the *Bulletin* school of writers that the bush is the major shaping instrument of the Australian identity, and that bush values are Australian values. In his last two novels, written after the war, a more pessimistic note prevails in his depiction of both character and landscape. The malevolent atmosphere of these grim alternatives to the romantic pictures of the bush or the tropics and the nightmarish qualities of their plots, the sufferings of their central characters, move back into the world of Barbara Baynton.

Wenz became even more keenly involved in Australian literature after the war, reading widely, following the debates from afar, and taking an interest in the activities of the Fellowship of Australian Writers and the Australian Literature Society. He corresponded with Dorothea Mackellar and Chris Brennan, admired Katharine Susannah Prichard, and developed friendships with Nettie Palmer, G. B. Lancaster, Miles Franklin and Frank

Clune. Perhaps his experience of Europe and his long absence from Australia during the war acted as a kind of watershed for him: he would have been out of sympathy with a lot of what was happening in French literature after the war, having no way of responding to modernism or the surrealist movement for example, and he was no doubt relieved to be able to retreat to the comfortable Australian position of isolationism.

Both as a person and as a writer he had already taken up a pretty strong option on Australia long before the war: his early use of the pen-name 'Paul Warrego' is more than just a superficial sign here, I think. In any case, during the last ten years of his life he seems to have embraced more definitely than before an Australian identity. He had his books included several times in exhibitions to promote Australian literature organised by the ALS; he tried increasingly to have his novels and stories translated into English and sought interest in publishing them here; he made a number of approaches to educational authorities to have some of his works included in school and university curricula. (He did achieve at least some success here: the University of Western Australia set *L'Echarde* as part of the French course in 1937.)

All of this could be seen merely as the attempt of an old man to ensure the survival of his reputation before dying; but it seems to me, rather, to be an attempt to secure a reputation *in* Australia, and *as an Australian*, or at least an Australian-identified, author—and not just 'a French writer with local interest.'

How then are we to define Paul Wenz's identity? A. G. Stephens and Nettie Palmer, those two arbiters and theorists who were so prominent in the Australian literary discourse before World War II, had no trouble in defining his identity in relation to Australian literature. In a *Bulletin* review of Wenz's first book, *A l'autre bout du monde*, A. G. Stephens wondered as early as 1906 whether, for Wenz, 'his new country is supplanting the old'. He went on to say:

One admires the skill with which Mr Wenz has taken the familiar motives of Australian story [. . .] and given them fresh weight and currency in another language.

He also praised Wenz's Australian stories for showing 'a keen appreciation of bush character'.[1] As late as 1954, Vance Palmer, in his book *The Legend of the Nineties*, could cite one of Wenz's stories as capturing the essence of the typical bush attitude of quiet, determined courage. So there was never any doubt among those who knew his work that Wenz could speak with an identifiably Australian voice, even if that voice did speak in French.

Nettie Palmer had the benefit of knowing the range of Wenz's work and of having met him personally. In an article in the *Brisbane Courier*, 1928, she was the first to point to his privileged status as a cultural intermediary:

Even though Paul Wenz is intimately Australian, and could sign one of his early books 'Paul Warrego' [. . .] his quality as a Frenchman means certain gains, too [. . .] Paul Wenz has looked long and steadily at the Australia he knows, both at long and at short range. The distance in his view gives proportion and clarity of outline—perhaps an over-diagrammatic clarity, but certainly an interesting one.[2]

She develops the point further in a 'Red Page' article in the *Bulletin* in 1929:

Paul Wenz is a French-Australian. He passes from his birthplace, Rheims, to a sheep station in the heart of New South Wales. In his Australian books there is no trace of Rheims except that his French is sound. His eyes are all the time on Australia which he sees in perspective and reduces to a few simple lines [. . .]

---

[1] The *Bulletin*, 21 June 1906.

[2] The *Brisbane Courier*, 3 November 1928.

Wenz's landscapes are from the most haggard interior; his persons are the most cynical, if the most childlike, of bushmen, usually bearing some simple name like Jim or Jack, and without any past or future. His bush settlements are those of Lawson's more arid stories. The bushmen whom Tom Collins in *Such is Life* saw from within, hearing them talk and think, Wenz draws as silhouettes with bizarre, decorative effect.

She goes on to praise him for having been able 'to use the essential rhythms of Australian life'.[3]

In another 'Red Page' article later the same year, Palmer has no hesitation in hailing the contribution of Wenz's writing to the evolving discourse of Australianness:

. . . the Australian writer is often frightened of doing more than mention a place; he is always being warned against the use of local colour. [. . .] Let us now praise Paul Wenz for his vivid pictures of a boundary-rider's hut near the Darling, Louis Stone for his slum streets and his harbour pictures, Dowell O'Reilly for the vignettes of Sydney scenes. [. . .] Let us praise them; they are giving us much that is very difficult to give for the first time; they are also saving the coming Australian novelists from having the worst 'nuisance of a job before them'.[4]

As critics of Australianness, Stephens and the Palmers are clear-sighted and thoughtful enough to be able to distinguish between the superficial jottings in a mere visitor's notebook, and what they see as the genuine, and perhaps unique, contribution of Wenz to the evolving Australian discourse. Nettie Palmer's perceptive observation that 'Paul Wenz's books, written for Paris, provide us with a sort of telescope through which we get one European view of ourselves'[5] points up the true function of Wenz as that

---

[3] The *Bulletin*, 13 March 1929.

[4] The *Bulletin*, 12 June 1929.

[5] The *Bulletin*, 13 March 1929.

of being a French-Australian author with, if you like, a foot firmly planted on either side of that crucial hyphen. He is speaking from the privileged position of 'interculturality', or, if you prefer, intertextuality in a very full sense. We can perhaps only today really contemplate or comprehend such a voice, as we are only now beginning to recognise and admit into the pantheon of Australian Literature those parts of it that were not originally written in English. Paul Wenz can well be seen as one of the first of our multicultural writers.

Maurice Blackman

DIARY OF A NEW CHUM

I was asked to a fancy dress ball at the Perkins', and for some unaccountable reason I accepted. As a rule this sort of distraction does not appeal to me. I do not understand the craving that makes people pretend they are Romeo, Lady Teazle, a clown, or a French cook for a few hours every winter.

I found myself the only Mexican in the motley crowd, and was soon introduced to a French peasant, who had taken the opportunity of displaying pretty arms and very shapely legs. She was dancing beautifully, and proved a pleasant partner. After several waltzes, I was allowed to take her to supper.

We had some champagne; not much, but it went to my head, and I felt suddenly hopelessly in love with the French peasant.

I am not what is termed a drinker, though I have a glass of wine or whisky when I feel so inclined; but never before did champagne make such an idiot of me. My partner looked certainly fetching, while sipping the last drop out of her glass. But why, between two bites into a paté de foie gras sandwich, I should have proposed to her is more than I ever will understand.

She took the thing very coolly, and without any of the 'too sudden' look about her. She simply asked if I really meant it. I said, 'Yes,' and was accepted.

While walking home in the cold, crisp air of that early morning, I did not realise that something had happened.

When the bright sunshine woke me I felt as must feel the man who has just spent his first night in gaol, and the terrible reality dawned upon me with mighty force.

Here I was, barely twenty-two, engaged to Miss Mary Smith, an acquaintance of four hours.

Joe came into my room. He had tried to speak to me at the ball last night, but I was too much enraptured with my French peasant. The girl, said my friend, was a dangerous creature. She had had a fellow up for breach of promise some six months ago, and had extracted £800 out of the faithless one. I learned a lot more about my . . . fiancée—a lot I would have liked to have known yesterday.

Joe showed me plainly what a fool I was, and what a narrow escape I had the chance to have.

My mind was made up. I took my passage for Australia. I wrote her a note, telling her that I had suddenly to go on a long trip, and mentioned Australia.

My packing was done in record time, and when that same night the boat left the wharf a German band played 'The Girl I Left Behind Me.'

I threw them half-a-crown.

Most people seem to guess I am a new arrival. They call me a New Chum. I asked them how they could tell. One said by my gloves and stick, another by my clothes and my face, another by my English; for, it appears, I have a London 'accent'. These Australians were kind, and showed me round Sydney. There is a touch of protection in their kindness, but their welcome and hospitality are pleasing to a stranger. There is no great formality out here, and as soon as a man has caught your name, he offers you a drink.

Sydney harbour? Yes, I have seen it. I have admired it, but gasworks, advertisements, and rows of hideous houses are spoiling parts of it.

Girls? Yes, they are pretty, have small feet and big eyes— hard-working eyes I should call them. My first impression is that Australian women are far above the men in point of looks and intellect. I believe I am right, for some women have endorsed my opinion. And they ought to know.

When I left Sydney by train last night it was too dark to see the country. After a broken sleep I woke up early this morning, impatient to have a glimpse of the Australian bush. I saw plains

18

dotted with trees and at times looking like a big park. Sheep, cattle, and horses were grazing along the line. Some of them ran away for a hundred yards; others scarcely took any notice of us, but went on grazing. The landscape is strange to me, and unlike anything I have seen.

The colouring is all subdued; the green of the eucalyptus is nearly grey; the sky is of a very pale blue; the grass is dead yellow. The clumps of dark green pines and the reddish soil are the only notes to relieve this neutrality. Dry creeks and gullies, rivers with more sand than water, are passed now and then.

The horse tied up under the hot sun, the man who constantly keeps the flies moving round his face, remind one that summer is approaching. The trees resemble each other, the houses we pass are all of the same pattern, and miles of posts complete the monotony. The dead trees standing with their contorted bare limbs add a note of sadness. The amount of wire they use in this country is incredible, the waste of firewood lying about is enormous.

The owner of the station read my letter of introduction, and straight away offered me ten shillings a week. I never expected any wages at first, and told Mr Telford that my knowledge of woolly and hairy quadrupeds was rather scant. I could tell a sheep when I saw one amongst a lot of goats, but that was all. The owner insisted on my accepting the ten shillings, so that he could swear at me without scruple when my work should require any sort of encouragement. I like his way of dealing.

Could I ride? Well, I had been on a horse or two at home, but from what I hear, my education will have to start afresh up here.

It has started, this very morning.

They brought into the yard a horse, saddled and bridled. The animal looked somewhat expectant, so did half-a-dozen men perched on the top rails.

The brute would not stand quiet while I was trying to get into the saddle. It took me over five minutes to put my foot in the stirrup. Then it was time wasted, as the horse flung me some distance as soon as I raised myself from the ground. Result: a sprained shoulder.

Australians are fond of practical jokes. This was a sample of them yesterday. I now learn that the horse they gave me to try had not been ridden for six months. Neither the boss, nor his brother, would have ridden him for anything. The boss was sorry to have allowed the joke. The men came to my help when they saw me stretched in the yard, but they had a good laugh first. One day or another the horse joke will hit them hard when they have to bury a New Chum who could not ride.

I had to own I could not crack a stockwhip. This seem to be a terrible gap in a man's education out here, so I decided to learn. Bill, the stockman, offered to teach me. He said it was very easy, and started to show me. For half a minute the long lash hissed angrily and exploded in the air. It certainly looked easy—at a distance. Flushed with pride, and with a twinkle in his eyes, Bill handed me the weapon.

I knew it was loaded, but made up my mind to show a bold face and have a try. I bravely took the whip and split the atmosphere without much result except that I nearly cut myself in halves. Bill was certainly inclined to indulgence, and, always smiling, told me to persevere. I had another try; this time I got better. My teacher was growing excited, and was coming closer and closer to prompt me. Suddenly, the whip hit him fair across the face. He at once lost all interest in my education, and went away holding his cheeks.

Last night I had a stroll, admiring the sky riddled with stars. Passing near the yards, I noticed half-a-dozen calves shut in a pen, looking lonely and disconsolate, while their mothers from outside were answering their plaintive calls. I have always been fond of animals; they have, most of them my sympathy. These calves had certainly, so I opened the gate and let them join their mothers. The meeting was touching. I went to bed feeling I had done a good deed.

From what I gather this morning, and from what the cowboy explains in forcible language, it is advisable to master one's feelings at times, and to let the little calves call their mothers till 7.30 in the morning.

The softness of heart towards animals from which I suffer is evidently misunderstood here, both by man and beast. My horse, I noticed, had a sore eye, which the flies were constantly worrying. When I got to the creek I bathed the eye as well as I could, then managed with some difficulty to bandage it with my wet handkerchief. So far, the steed, which was a quiet one, seemed thankful, and did not object to looking like Don Quixote's Rosinante. But when I got into the saddle, the bandage somehow became loose, the horse bolted, and did a quarter of a mile in very quick time. I succeeded in stopping him, and decided not to let my feelings carry me away any more.

Many and varied are the duties of the New Chum. I have been here only a couple of months, but have learned many things I never dreamed of. Poisoning rabbits with water and arsenic is one of the branches of the profession in which I am getting fairly proficient. In itself the art is easy to get hold of, but it requires nerves—olfactory nerves.

Branding of calves is, of course, painful to me, to say nothing of the calves. The peppery dust of the yards, the choked bellowing of the victims, the smell of burning hide, made me nearly faint the first time.

Cutting chaff by hand power I call very monotonous. It takes such a lot of chaff and dust to fill one bag. Digging post-holes does not maintain its novelty very long. As for cutting Bathurst burrs, I have been at it a week already. So far, I feel satisfied that the brain of a New Chum can stand a good strain.

Mat and Syd (I don't believe they own any other names) are camping with me on a creek twenty-five miles from the homestead. Every morning after breakfast we leave the shady timber and ride about in a treeless paddock of about 10,000 acres. We take our lunch and waterbags, and go the whole day from one Bathurst burr to another. When they are growing scattered our horses stop on their own accord, and we wield the hoe without dismounting. Often we strike patches of half an acre or more, so we get off and cut burrs for hours.

Yesterday the boss rode out to see how we were getting on. He told us it was 110 degrees in the shade. I am sure he did not get his information in this paddock.

I find that the less brain a job requires the more one's brain works. This sort of work is purely mechanical; monkeys could be trained to do it. During the long lonely hours memories come back in a stream, some still fresh, some long forgotten, covered with the dust of years, and bearing the scent of dead leaves. Some are sweet and some are bitter. The calmness of everything stirs the imagination, and faces of faraway friends rise from the streaming ground like mirages. The same feeling holds me when I ride for long hours along the fences. The step of the horse, the ceaseless creaking of the saddle rock the mind into a half-sleep, accompanied by dreams.

Before sunset we go back to the camp, and while the billy boils and the meat goes through a process resembling cooking, we have a wash in the creek, and soon forget that we are tired. By the time we have finished the meal round the fire the stars are out, and the glorious night is upon us.

I love these evenings, and fully enjoy the pipe I smoke while watching the fire. Above our heads the big gums blot out the stars with the dark, uncertain form of their foliage, and while I listen to the frogs in the creek, to the curlew, and to all these strange noises of a strange land, Mat and Syd talk horses.

My two mates are authorities on horses; they know the equine history from the horse of Troy up. The dates of the battle of Hastings, of the discovery of America they have forgotten, or perhaps never knew. The kings they know have quaint names;

the victories were mostly won in the months of October and November; the battlefields not far from Melbourne or Sydney. Their memory is simply astonishing. They know a long list of horses' names taken from all languages of the world.

Not being a racing man, their knowledge is wasted upon me, and my conversation has, I am sure, little attraction for them. They are good fellows, somewhat sorry for me that I was not born in Australia. They are obliging, and quite willing to forget at times what I am. I should think that theirs is a happy lot, for they live in a perpetual hope of becoming rich men suddenly. Their Providence spells Tattersall, and when their number will come out—well, they will own racehorses!

My bed is under a big gum tree, from which opossums shake leaves and twigs upon me while they are playing in the light of the moon. My mattress is made of gum leaves, my pillow of boots and clothes. My alarm clock consists of swarms of flies; it works too early for my taste. The sunrise is no doubt beautiful, but as a rule we are not in a fit frame of mind to admire all its beauty. This is why sunsets are described much oftener and much better than sunrises.

My mates told me there are many snakes about. I ought to have been thankful for the volunteered information, but it spoiled my first nights. The smallest wood-bug crawling amongst the dry grass represented to my searching eyes a tiger snake of tremendous proportions.

Mat and Syd have also described venomous black spiders, with a red dot on their back, which bite you into lunacy inside ten minutes. They mentioned casually bulldog ants and centipedes big enough to give a New Chum the horrors.

Syd owns a stockwhip made of kangaroo leather, and is very proud of it. He has brought it with him to the camp, although it can't be of much use to him for cutting burrs. Last night, after the long yarns about snakes, we went to bed. While I was undressing I noticed one brute half hidden under my bed. I jumped back and sang out to the others. They never moved, just laughed.

In a moment I had my hoe, and with a mighty blow nearly cut in halves—Syd's stockwhip.

My mates were still laughing with all their might when I brought them the spoil. Mat went on laughing. I joined him. Syd was swearing, and for part of the night cursed New Chums in general.

Mat is naturally very vain; his vanity knows no limit; he believes that he can cook. Tonight he has given us what they call 'flap-jacks'; it really does not deserve such a high-sounding name. A flap-jack is made by first spilling some water on some flour (or the flour on the water, I don't remember which), then when it has been worked to the consistency of putty two months old, you flatten the thing with your hands, and drop it into boiling fat. Afterwards comes the dangerous part of the operation—you have to eat it.

I am wondering whether 'flap-jacks' are yet another joke!

Sunday! No burrs to cut for twenty-four hours, which makes today doubly a day of rest. I have to break the Sabbath all the same, and do some washing. This is a work entirely novel to me. What a lot of things they don't teach you at school!

I found a dead tree, half in the creek, half out of it, and beautifully adapted, I thought, to serve as a scrubbing board; so I started on a pair of white moleskin trousers. It certainly takes a lot of soap to get anything like a result, and before I had finished one side of the garment the creek was soapy for yards round me. I must say that I had to give an extra scrubbing to one leg, as I had left half a plug of tobacco in the pocket.

When I felt satisfied that one side was done, I found the other all green with the slime and mud which caked my scrubbing board, so I had to finish the job in the creek. I reflected that we go through life seeing people doing washing, and we never realise what this means till we have to try ourselves. There is much more in washing clothes than you ever dreamt of.

The mail arrives here only once a week—on Saturdays. I have received a letter today which I have expected with dread for some time.

Mary Smith does not write a very good hand, but she can write six pages on end. Of course, I knew that men do not understand the love of a woman. Goodness knows, they have been trying long enough, but still they don't know what it is worth.

I was also aware that we are a selfish lot, that I was no exception. But I was not aware that the woman who knew me could not live away from me. I felt I must be a terrible nuisance to be in her mind day and night, to follow her everywhere like a ghost.

I agreed with her that I ought to be ashamed never to have written her a single word for three long months, after having left without even saying goodbye. But what I felt most keenly about in the letter was her mentioning coming out to Australia.

This promise decided me to answer her letter, a thing I did not mean to do at first. I told her in three pages that I would dread to see her in this lonely land, far away from civilisation, risking her life every day, in a country teeming with snakes and cannibals, under a fierce sun. I put in a few more venomous spiders and centipedes, some awful malarias and jungle fevers.

And when I read over the letter I was sorry I was not a born liar, otherwise I would not have wished to kick myself as I did.

Miss Murphy is the only young woman on this station. She is the governess, and looks after the boss's children. When I arrived here first, I thought her the plainest woman I ever had seen. In fact, I never knew a woman could be so plain and live. I suppose some faces are like tea on board ship—you get used to them because there is nothing else. Anyhow, now I can look at her during meals without breaking anything.

The poor lady has no idea, I am sure, that she is far from pretty. She looks at herself in the dining room mirror opposite her seat at the table. She sports brooches and ribbons; smiles and makes eyes. Providence has done well to endow us with such a powerful imagination, otherwise we would commit suicide, dozens of us at a time. Miss Murphy is, I believe, silently admired by Thomson, the bookkeeper. I even suspect Thomson of writing poetry for her in the store, while cockroaches run upon the wall and mice have a meeting in the 'sultana' case.

The station owns a pet ram, and is proud of the ownership. Why they should be I cannot understand. The brute is ugly, covered up to its wicked eyes with a dense greasy fleece, which seem three sizes too big. It is called Philip, eats all sorts of things, and takes notice of everything. Yesterday, while I was going to the office, Philip took notice of me, and came straight in my direction with his head down. I was able to catch him by the horns and stop his impetus, but as soon as I let him go he insisted on aiming at my shin bones. After five minutes of a miniature bullfight, I had to take refuge upon a small stump just to see what Philip would do. Philip calmly waited, keeping his eyes on me. I wished something interesting would happen to draw the beast's attention somewhere else, but I was everything in the world to Philip just now. The stump was small, and was getting uncomfortable, when Miss Murphy called me to reach the children's ball, which had lodged on the roof of the verandah. Philip seemed to understand what was wanted of me. He followed as soon as I left the stump, and in spite of my smart 'feint,' knocked me down from behind.

Miss Murphy burst into a tactless laugh. She is really awfully plain when she laughs!

The cook is a greasy individual of a versatile turn of mind. Before handling pots and pans he was a sailor, then a miner. Boiled leg of mutton, hot and cold, roast ditto, cold or hot, seem to be the *plats de résistance* of his variety show. He has a weakness for blancmange and plum duff. The boss and his wife seem satisfied with the menus, and everybody eats without protest mutton twenty-one times a week and very few vegetables.

The cook is a terrible smoker, and smokes terrible tobacco, which he cuts indifferently with a bread knife or a dessert knife. He is fond of talking about any subject, but racing and politics are the themes he really enjoys.

I have been wondering whether his mining days had anything to do with his last night's plum pudding, for I found in it several mineral specimens. One of them cost me a tooth.

This 'chef' is also a great reader, and devours pages after pages of literature. The food he likes for his brain is no blancmange by any means; it consists of very strongly curried novels like 'Ben's Plucky Pard of Silver Gulch,' or 'Juanita, the Mexican Deadly Queen.' I find that the men in the hut also appreciate these books very much.

Occasional visitors are a distraction in the bush, though sometimes people avail themselves too freely of Australian hospitality. Last night a man arrived on foot from Queensland—some 500 miles. His baggage consisted of a small hand bag, which might hold a suit of summer pyjamas, a hairbrush, and a toothbrush. He was dressed in a tourist Scotch tweed, and wore a brown bowler hat. The boss did not know at first what to make of him. He looked like what is vaguely called a gentleman, but a very dirty, unwashed gentleman. Mr Telford offered him some tea, and when he found the visitor had decided to have his dinner at the homestead, he broadly hinted at a bath. He took him to the outside bathroom, and gave him a full course of instruction—how to pull the string for a shower, how to fill the bath, and how to empty it. The visitor was assured that with due care the handling of the taps was without any danger. He seemed to take a certain amount of interest in the demonstration, and inspected the whole thing as if it were a new kind of machinery.

For reasons of his own he did not take a bath, though he arrived at the table with his hair wet and carefully parted.

Mrs Telford treated the man with her usual kindness in spite of his dirty collar and his generally neglected appearance. His conversation was interesting, and he told us of his trip from

Queensland with a certain amount of humour. Considering the hard time he must have had on the track, with no camping outfit and a brown bowler hat, he must be a plucky individual.

After dinner, while we were in the smoking room, the visitor consented to solve for us the mysteries of his profession. He was a bump reader. He offered Mr Telford there and then to read his bumps and his wife's for half-a-crown a piece, but the boss was not interested. The overseer had the bumps of his seven children read at family prices, and next morning the man in tweeds disappeared along the dusty track.

Yesterday the boss gave me a holiday in order to enable me to see the Cowlong races. Cowlong is a heap of jam tins, round which fifty people are living, or think they are. It consists chiefly of a pub, a police station, a store, and a church, for they drink, eat, get run in, and die just as in any other place. Why this spot exists, and how it does, seems an impossible problem—to a New Chum, anyhow. Nevertheless, there is the CJC, which meets twice a year.

The meeting was interesting, I must say. The grandstand looked like a roosting place. The 'buffet' was made of gum boughs. The weighing was done on the store scales. I don't suppose the horses had any idea about their ancestors, but they ran and jumped well enough to arouse excitement amongst some 150 spectators, who gambled and lost money cheerfully. That night when I left the place a few drunks crowded the verandah of the Harp of Erin, and things were getting jolly. The wooden lock-up, I was told, had barely standing room by nine o'clock that night.

I saw Charley 'in town' (Cowlong calls itself a town, so does any place which boasts of more than five houses). He never misses any 'function,' and seems to be a very popular man. He had a lot of friends, for he owns a generous heart, and all the money he earns is swallowed, literally, by these friends.

Charley, the rabbiter, has a story. To look at him one would not expect much interest in his past. He is a good-natured

28

individual. The main part of his profile has been utterly spoiled by years of spree. You certainly cannot realise that Charley will one day or another be Sir Charles——. He has never told a word of his history in cold blood, but has dropped some of its incidents at the Harp of Erin many a time. It appears that his father owns a beautiful estate in England. Charley, the heir to the title and to the property, was, when out of Oxford, destined to be the husband of a carefully chosen young lady. Charley had a mind of his own, and refused blankly to have his love affairs managed by anybody but himself. Sir James——showed the door to his son. Charley made use of it, and never even turned round to shut it. This was eight years ago.

Charley landed in Australia with no proverbial half-a-crown and a taste for drink, which rapidly developed. He worked off and on upon different stations, and has been here rabbiting for the last eighteen months.

One day I stopped at his camp, where a dozen dogs, of all colours and no breed, took loud notice of my arrival. Charley threw sticks and swore at them, then offered me a cup of tea, which I accepted. There was no sign of Oxford about him while he went on skinning his rabbits; but Sir Charles came out when he handed me the pannikin of tea and the sugar. His voice had suddenly changed to a gentler note while he acted the host, and his manners had become different at once. From what I could see, he lives very much like a blackfellow. His furniture is mostly bark and sticks. A frying pan and a billy are his cooking utensils. He seems fairly happy. All this shows how easily we go back to the Stone Age of life if we only get a chance.

Another visitor, this time an insurance agent, has fallen upon us yesterday. After a good meal at the homestead (which he illustrated with a lot of funny anecdotes), the agent started to buttonhole the household, from the boss down to the cook. Mr Telford did not believe in gambling with his life, and would not follow the agent's demonstration that if he died in ten years from now the company (the best in Australia) would give him back his money and a good lot besides.

Nobody at the homestead valued his life very much, so the agent directed his fire towards the men's huts. They had been warned in time, and were ready for the enemy.

The man entered the hut where seven pipes were smoking their hardest. 'Good evening, boys!' he said with his best smile. Some grunts responded, but nobody stirred. The agent was not discouraged; he started to tell them some choice yarns. The men did not laugh very loud, just as if they were afraid they might be charged for the funny stories. Nevertheless, they each took the cigar he was offering, and puffed away with their right elbow out, just to show him that they knew how to hold a cigar.

The system was fully explained, a system which just made it a joke to die in order to get the best of the company. But the men were either slow of intellect or would not grasp the beauty of the system. No end of figures, no amount of literature distributed for their perusal, could convince them. Besides, the cigars were getting short stumps, and some of the boys were tired. Syd was the first to disappear from the circle of listeners. Jim followed suit three minutes later. The agent was busy explaining to Mat how much he would get back when seventy-five years old. When he turned round he found the audience lessened by three. The four left were getting nervous, and each was hoping he would not be left alone to face the speaker.

The agent felt he was not appreciated. Two more disappeared, and soon after the Old Guard retreated in bad order.

Finding himself alone in front of the fireplace, the agent was seized with a sudden fit of anger, and words filled the hut like the smoke of his rotten cigars. In the bunks could be seen forms squirming under blue blankets. The man's language was getting too strong, even for the hut. Syd got up and told him to insure his face against accidents. The agent got out of the room. The men had another quiet smoke and a laugh.

The boss must have found my specialty, for he trusts me now with a lot of boundary riding. At first, some months ago, riding was a real pleasure to me. I still like it, but I feel less excited about it.

Riding is no doubt a very enjoyable exercise, but it seems to me it depends a lot on the company you are in and on the country you have to go through. Being by myself, and riding for eight hours along miles of wires in a paddock which is called the One Tree Paddock, will explain perhaps why I have become a little 'blasé' about the pigskin. The One Tree Paddock deserves its name, but flatters itself all the same. The lonely tree is there, but it has been dead for years.

To see a fence running in a perfectly straight line towards the horizon gives you an idea of the infinite, of the never-ending, which is nearly maddening.

During these lonely hours in the paddock I have caught myself reciting or singing aloud all I could gather out of my memory. When the spring came, and the flies were getting numerous, I had to stop declamation and singing, for I was swallowing some at each verse.

I have been told that people who live in the bush go mad at times. I can believe it. I have dreamt dreams with my eyes open. I have thought mad thoughts, and made plans foolish and impossible. And there is no sign of lunacy in my family.

The crow reminds you that you are awake; the rustling of its wings has the sweet 'frou-frou' of a woman's dress, its croak is the laugh of the devil. The kangaroo bounds weirdly in front of you, and the emu passes in a frantic and ridiculous gait.

Today I found in the corner of the paddock a sheep lying down. One eye had been taken out by the crows, who perched on the fence posts, resented my interference, and croaked angrily. The poor brute had been struggling during the torture, and two half-circles were scraped on the ground where it lay. The socket full of blood seemed to stare at the pale blue sky. The sight of it filled me with rage.

I did not even try to put the beast on its legs, but made up my mind to shorten its agony.

31

For the first time in my life I killed a sheep. My hand was trembling while the knife searched a good spot on the woolly throat, but the blade did its work well. I shut my eyes and set my teeth while I heard the life gurgling out of the gash. When I felt the body still and insensible I looked, and saw the pool of blood, beautiful in its colour under the bright sun.

It took me nearly half an hour to skin the sheep; it was not expert skinning, but it was hard work. I brought the skin to the station.

The boss looked at it, and never said a word. The boy inspected the spoil, and remarked that it was fairly rough. I know he showed it to some of the men. The exhibition made them wonder loudly.

As long as they live they won't know what it cost me to kill the poor brute, and their laughs will never counterbalance the awful pangs I felt when my knife first entered that skin.

Bill had a pup for sale—a beautiful pup. The pedigree of this infant dog was something to be proud of. The performances of the pup's parents, the prizes they had taken at shows, added considerably to the value of Algernon, which was for sale at three guineas. I thought the figure somewhat exaggerated, but Bill assured me that he had refused many offers already.

I know the sheepdog instinct is in him already. At six weeks old he works chickens in spite of angry hens. He is full of pluck, and barks at draught horses. Bill was finally willing to let me have him for £2, which he said was a real bargain.

Algernon, in spite of his alleged aristocratic origin, is nothing much to look at. He is black and tan, and as woolly as a bear. His fur has already been put through a severe test. Being of an exploring turn of mind, he went the other day roaming round the cask of molasses, which is badly leaking since the summer started. He took great interest in this cask, and managed to get his fur into one solid mass of molasses. To make things worse, he rolled several times in the dust, and then looked more like a lump of dirt than anything else. He did not appear to be worth £2 then. I spent a Sunday morning in melting Algy in three buckets of water and a quantity of soap. I got rid of most of the molasses and of the best part of his fur.

Being too young to be taken out in the run, he spends his days at the end of a long chain, which he twists to a fourth of its length. He manages now and then to slip his collar, and to practise on fowls. He varies the distraction by inspecting the boss's garden, and chasing ghosts amongst the best flower beds. He certainly likes to show off, and keeps the public eye on him.

Yesterday I thought he was ripe for a debut, so tied him at the end of a long cord in order to make him follow the horse. His first steps were not spontaneous; he let himself be dragged like a log of wood. He soon found out that the ordinary method of progress was best, but would not go straight; he was tacking all the time. He must have learned before the possibilities of a horse's hind legs, for he kept at a respectful distance, leaving no slack in the cord.

The horse resented being tied to a pup, and gave a sudden jerk, which nearly unsettled me. Algy gave also a jerk, and cantered in the direction of the homestead, trailing ten feet of rope behind him. Pedigreed animals seem hard to train.

By looking through the lists of passengers arriving from London by *S S Ortona*, I saw with horror the name of Miss M. Smith.

I know that thirty-one per cent of humanity is labelled Smith. Nevertheless I felt certain that the passenger in question is the very one I do not want to see in Australia—or anywhere else.

The boat called at Fremantle on the 16th; she would be in Sydney in a week. Danger was getting nearer. After some sleepless nights I decided to send a wire to Miss M. Smith.

'Where shall I meet you? Wire George. PO Hay.'

It was a bold move, but it took me a long time to write the line.

Two mails arrived. No answer. It was agony.

This morning the blow came down.

'Meet me Saturday, Coffee Palace, Sydney.—Smith.'

I told the boss I wanted to go down to Sydney—on business, not on pleasure—which was perfectly true.

My feelings were strangely mixed and hard to describe when I crossed the door mat of the Coffee Palace.

I inquired for Miss Smith, and gave the porter my card. He disappeared up the lift, leaving me in the hall looking at the picture of *The Battle of Trafalgar*. It seemed a long three minutes waiting. The porter came back, my card still in his hand. Miss Smith thought there must be some mistake. My name was unknown to her.

My heart leapt with joy—like the boy who has just escaped a private meeting with the headmaster. I could scarcely believe my luck.

I turned on my heels and made for the door, but before I had gone two steps the porter called me back. I found myself face to face with a very pretty girl.

She timidly introduced herself as Miss Madeline Smith, just out from London. She answered my wire, believing it would reach her cousin George Sharp. I began to feel sorry I was not that cousin, for the Miss Smith I had before me was a very sweet creature.

We both laughed at the mistake. Personally, I thought it a very good joke.

Shearing has started. I was curious to see what it was like, for they have been talking about it for the last two months. This morning at 8.30, after the roll call, the engine's whistle blew. The men were ready and set to work. The gates of the pens banged, and the shed was filled with a buzzing noise. The machines cut their tracks through the dense wool, and the fleeces were peeled off like the skin from huge potatoes. The sheep appeared white as snow. There was a red streak here and there, but a dab from the tarboy soon changed it into a dirty splash.

My particular job was weighing the bales and branding them, so I had time at first to watch the whole process with both eyes. The first bale I branded was not an unqualified success—too

34

much ink on my brush, the stencil plate somewhat crooked. The boss and the two pressers were looking at me while I was branding, a thing I object to when I do some delicate work. The boss said nothing; his silence was painful to hear.

The following bales were branded straight and neat, without a smudge. I felt like a kid doing the first page of a new copy book, and, like a kid, had all my fingers full of ink. This job is going to last five weeks, so I shall have time to learn branding bales thoroughly.

Shearing, like most things in this world, is interesting at first, then it gets monotonous. Wet weather gave us a spell now and then; finally, the last sheep was shorn, and the last bale branded.

The greasy, grumbly shearer had a thorough wash, left his working clothes to adorn the surroundings of his hut, and appeared dressed for town. These shearers are suddenly different men. They have a smile and a joke ready for everybody while they wait for their turn to pocket their cheque.

The traces the shearers and rouseabouts leave behind them afford matter for a study of their gastronomic tastes. A big heap of jam tins, pickles, vinegar, and tomato sauce bottles, all of a good brand, are a proof that they are epicures. The general appearance of the inside of the hut leads one to suppose that tidiness is not a virtue amongst them. Packs of cards, worn-out boots and clothes, straw, empty cigarette packets, old newspapers, and letters, etc., are all left for us to burn in a big stack. Numerous slush lamps, the product of local industry, are also conspicuous. A slush lamp is a contrivance which smokes and smells a lot, but gives little light. It was invented during the Stone Age, and has never been improved since.

We had some distractions during shearing. One afternoon arrived a rattling trap drawn by the shadow of a horse, in charge of an old man and a boy. The whole turnout was labelled 'The World's Entertainment Company.' The rumour soon spread that a performance would be given that night.

There was a good house, and an appreciative one; the program was full of variety.

It opened with a song, accompanied by a concertina. Then the boy gave an exhibition of step dancing, after which the old man recited 'The Charge of the Light Brigade.' I had heard the masterpiece before, but this man presented it in quite a new way. His pipe never left his mouth during the Charge, and in the thickest of the fight he coolly stopped to relight it.

The next number was the magic lantern. We saw successively the 'Death of Mary Queen of Scots', 'The Discovery of Australia', 'The Kelly Gang', a 'Portrait of Deeming' (the famous murderer), 'Tarcoola' and the 'Royal Family'. 'Tarcoola' and 'The Kelly Gang' divided the honours between them.

A gramophone ground a few comic songs and played the National Anthem out of a wornout, cracked record. Few of the men had cash, so they put their names down, and the sum of 28s was collected.

Thomson, the bookkeeper, is more than ever in love with Miss Murphy. The warming up of his love can be seen growing apace. His ties are tied more carefully, and are of tender hue. His hair is parted mathematically and smoothed down, till it looks as if he had his head japanned. Thomson is not better looking than the ordinary man you meet, but I suppose all people in love fancy themselves a bit.

Yesterday being Saturday, Thomson was very busy giving out rations, cleaning the store, and counting scalps brought in by Charley and the other rabbiters.

This operation is both tedious and odorous; the scalps are sometimes a fortnight old, and the dead kittens are very dead.

Thomson was on the store verandah counting the 768th scalp, when Miss Murphy happened to pass quite close, back from a walk with the children. The bookkeeper lifted his eyes and was ready for a cheerful greeting, but Miss Murphy only lifted her little nose and passed without a sign of recognition. The incident was, like the smell of scalps, far-reaching, and brought down

36

a big cloud on Thomson's life for over a week, but this was a long time for Miss Murphy to stay without feeling or hearing somebody's admiration; so they made it up somehow. Thomson came to life again, and once more whistled merrily to the cockroaches in the store.

Christmas! I am told by the almanac that this is Christmas Day. The thermometer marks 101 degrees under the verandah, and the flies are swarming everywhere. You would expect that in Australia old Father Christmas would be allowed to go without his furs, with scarcely anything on. But imagination is hard to kill; the poor man in everybody's mind as well as on the Christmas cards is obliged to be in full uniform.

We have a Christmas tree, and have to face a plum pudding just as solid as the genuine English article. The fat goose is there, too!

O, for just one square yard of real snow! One breath of cold, snappy wind, loaded with the scent of pines! If I live a hundred years in Australia the 25th of December will be the day before the 26th, but never Christmas.

All the same it was fairly gay today till after the long dinner, when most of us felt sleepy.

I noticed that Thomson had a sprig of paper mistletoe (paper mistletoe, think of it!) hanging from one of the beams of his store; I noticed, also, that Miss Murphy had to go to the store to get some ink. It took her some twenty minutes to get it!

I never knew what thirst meant till I came to this country. What I had taken for thirst before was only make-believe compared to the desire you have here to drown yourself in cold water. The weather has been keeping hot lately—107 degrees in the shade and about 95 degrees in the moonlight! The result is that we do not sleep much at night, but pass our time hanging on to a waterbag.

We are four in the bachelors' quarters, and often meet on our verandah at all hours of the night, saying a word to the waterbag. We each have our own hanging in front of our door. Thomson, who is a teetotaller, has the biggest. It must have been made to order.

When I go round the fence of the One Tree Paddock, which takes about eight hours, without seeing a drop of water, I am nursing a beautiful thirst. The long hours pass, the saddle groans and creaks, the horse walks like a machine under the terrible sun. Then after the gate is passed the beast starts cantering on its own accord, for we are getting near the river. The dog (which now follows without a hawser) has suddenly disappeared. I find him swimming and pretending to swallow the whole river. The horse steps carefully down the bank, stretches his neck and gently takes a long drink. The third beast goes on its knees, throws its hat off, and plunges its face in the water.

The gay warbling of the magpie, the sad, hellish note of the crow during the day, the cheerful whistle of the wagtails, the lonely cry of the curlew at night, are the things which impressed me most at first in the Australian bush. What I have seen and heard about this country leads me to believe that it is a land of contrasts. Fine seasons are followed by awful droughts. When rain has been plentiful and herbage is knee-high, the fire sweeps the plain as soon as summer comes. The bushman is always fighting something—seasons, pests or diseases—and this continual fight has made of him a plucky philosopher, a man who takes things as they come, since they insist in coming so often when they are not wanted. The Australian is also a gambler at heart; he has to be, for everything seems to be a gamble in the bush. When he sees his sheep dying all over the paddocks, when he is sick of skinning swollen carcases, he thinks he will get better luck next year. When crop after crop is a failure, he tears the ground once more with his plough, and says to himself, 'Better luck next time!'

During a prosperous season, if you ask him how things are with him, he will, as a rule, answer, 'Not too bad!' Being a gambler, he is superstitious, and seems frightened lest the Fates hear him say, 'Very good!' And when things are bad he will answer, 'Not too good!' just as if he were expecting worse, and were ready for it, too.

The bush is sad; the bushman is sad, too. His face is lit up by beautiful big eyes, deep, like sailors' eyes, and, like them, always looking far ahead, and then they will see things the New Chum cannot see. All Australian Aborigines and animals have beautiful eyes. There must be something in the atmosphere which dilates the pupils.

What I miss most in this country is a forest of big shady trees, the dark green foliage, the running water, and the moss. I miss the hedges and the old stone walls covered with ivy. I miss the snow and the ice, which cracks like powdered sugar under the skates. But, then, wherever we live, we miss something, and the Australian would freeze in our snow just as we gasp under his sun.

Sunday night. Why is this night always sad with me? Ever since my school days I have disliked Sunday nights. Then I probably regretted the short holiday, and had in perspective the French class first thing on Monday morning. But the feeling will stay with me all my life. It takes me hours to go to sleep. I am thinking of home, and I can plainly hear, about eight o'clock at night, the church bells thousands of miles away. And now, a curlew is crying not a hundred yards from my room. It makes the night sadder still.

Charley has received an important letter from a Sydney solicitor. His father is dead. So Charley the rabbiter is now Sir Charles——.

He left the station yesterday. The news of his father's death seems to have told on him. His face was stern, and his eyes seemed to stare into the gone past, into years of life and love wasted by him. He shook hands with all of us, gave his dogs to Bill, and asked him to look after them. After he had gone some yards he turned round, for he heard Ginger-beer, his pet slut, barking furiously and pulling on the chain. He called out to Bill to let her loose. Mad with joy, the little beast ran after him, and, while he was patting her, he lifted his hat once more to bid us farewell, and they were gone.

We heard from the mailman that Charley had gone straight through the township without even looking at the 'Harp of Erin.' He camped near the river till the coach passed.

Old Jones is the oldest hand on the place; he has a fine head, with long white hair and beard, which they say were one time closely shaven. Some assume that his heavy way of walking comes from the irons he used to wear round his ankles, for he was sent out here for having stolen six geese. Whether it is true or not, Jones is a fine fellow, and everybody treats him with respect. He does odd jobs, looks after the dogs, and drives old Trooper at the horseworks when the tanks want filling.

Jones loves his pipe; I never have seen him without it. I have even found him asleep with the black briar in his mouth.

Trooper is a horse which knows enough to be something else. He can open any gate, and has tried with success every patent gate-opener on the place. He has a knack of going where horses ought not to go. He was found once partly in the harness room. He got jammed in the door, and for some time could not make up his mind whether to get in or out. Finally, he decided to retreat, taking away with him one side of the building.

Jack, the carpenter, is the ideal type of a man, who can make furniture out of packing cases; candlesticks, soap dishes, flower vases, lanterns and other things out of kerosene tins. I should like to know what the man cannot do. He repairs boots and kitchen utensils, mends chairs, watches and waggons, does some blacksmithing, cleans guns and chimneys. Nothing frightens him. He would fix up a typewriter if you asked him, or try to mend a broken thermometer. I wanted to see how far his pluck would go, so went to his shop this morning to have a yarn with him. He was busy making a new head for Lizzie's doll. The new head

40

was a bit out of proportion with the body, but it had eyes, nose, mouth and ears, all complete, and a short crop of hair cunningly done with a piece of rabbit skin stuck on with glue.

I quite solemnly asked Jack if he thought he could make a piano. He never flinched, and was ready for me. 'Maybe I could, but it'll take some working; only them notes would be the trouble— such a lot of them, and the wires, too.' He thought that nice redgum, well polished and varnished, would look well. He said he might tackle it one day or another. I daresay he will.

Araminta, Lizzie's doll, had to be rechristened, for, according to the owner, she was not a bit like the old doll before the accident, so she became Ivy. But Ivy's life was short. She was left in the sun, and her yellow box head not being well seasoned, split right across. One of the pups saw the last of Ivy.

I have not been long enough out here to know much about sheep, but I have studied them on many occasions. My first question to myself was, 'Are sheep as brainless as they are said to be generally?' Philip, the pet ram which I personally know, seems to have a fair amount of reasoning power (he knew I would have to get off that stump) and a good share of will (he would not be satisfied till he got me). Pet lambs are no fools, and know a lot of things, especially a bottle with a quill stuck into the cork.

I have often watched a mob going through a gate. No two faces are alike. Many of them remind one of people one knows. I have seen the old ewe with a curly fringe on her forehead and a cunning look in her eyes. I had met that ewe before— on two legs. I spotted a big, fat wether with a silly eye, his face adorned with side whiskers and full of self-conceit. I knew a butler exactly like it. Some look happy with their lot, some seem sorry they are just sheep. But I like most the ewe, proud of the white lamb who worries the life out of her and who nearly knocks her down at meal times. I admire her when she suddenly turns round to face the dog and stamps her foot.

The first sundowner I met interested me. He told me he walked from Queensland looking for work and not finding any. He was a young man, strong and full of life. His story reached my heart. I gave him some tobacco and a shilling. He called me a gentleman. The next morning he had left the place. So had a roast leg of mutton, a waterbag, and some washing.

Since that time I do not encourage swaggies to call me a gentleman any more, though they most of them come from the Queensland border. My heart has become callous, and unless the tramp is an old or feeble man I consider sundowners lazy philosophers, rambling Diogenes who are showing people that Australia is a country where anyone can live by merely moving his legs. They do not use their biceps. A good pair of calves is all they want. Most men work to get a living. The swaggie walks to get the same result.

One of them camped on the river for weeks, catching fish, which he exchanged at the store for some tobacco, tea, or jam. Last Sunday I passed his camp, when he called me for a pipeful of tobacco. His own story came out with the first whiffs, and before I had time to light my pipe he had started to unfold his biography. He said he had been a clerk in a Sydney office at 30s. per week. He fell in love with a girl; she fell in love with him. One day she changed her mind. He nearly lost his, and when she married the other man he took to drink. Drink took him by the hand and led him on the tracks, where he has impressed the nails of his boots for the last ten years.

He has become a woman hater, never goes within coo-ee of a female if he can help it; never drinks at a pub where there is a woman behind the bar.

The man is not old, but his hair has gone grey, and his face has deep lines. He spoke quietly, without passion, and seemed reconciled with his lot. A few hooks for his fishing and some tobacco seem to be all he wants, till he gets enough money to spend at the nearest hotel.

The boss sent me to O'Mealy, the selector, to give him notice about lamb marking. I was careful in opening O'Mealy's gate, for it looked a delicate and fragile structure. In spite of all my precaution, it fell in three pieces. The patching up was done under difficulties, for two dogs were barking furiously while approaching towards me. A dirty child flew into the house, leaving his toys behind—a sheep's head and a jam tin.

Mrs O'Mealy received me from the verandah, buttoning a pink blouse. Her skirt was not long enough to hide the bare fact that she had no stockings, though she had boots. I guessed it was not her day at home. Nevertheless she showed me into the 'drawing room,' asking me to wait till she called her husband. I had a minute to inspect the drawing room; it was ample. The piano took my breath; it had the place of honour, and was loaded with photos in plush and hand-painted frames. The floor disappeared under opossum and rabbit skins; the chairs were draped with 'art' muslin and ribbons.

O'Mealy came in, said good day, and made some remarks about the state of the atmosphere. He received the message I delivered with marked interest. He invited me to play a 'toone' on his piano. I had to own my complete ignorance. He seems very proud of the instrument, which he considers as a drawing room piece of furniture more than anything else; for nobody in the house can play it.

He would have introduced me to the child, the pigs and the cows, had I not hinted that I had a good way to ride. He has fifty acres under cultivation. The same fifty acres have stood the process for the last eleven years. Sometimes they give a harvest, but not often. O'Mealy has only a small flock (a few wethers and a fair number of lambs). His selection is a poor bit of country. Still, the man lives; he even owns a piano. Mystery!

The boss told me tonight that it was no mystery at all. It was only sheepstealing. And him so pleasant and so polite to talk to! I hope that he will utilise the proceeds of his next transaction in buying a half a dozen pairs of 'warranted fast dye' for Mrs O'Mealy.

I had to ride forty miles to see the dentist, for I have damaged another tooth while eating peas two days ago. I must have struck a petrified one. The dentist, the only one in this town, was out shooting, so I had to wait till next morning, which gave me an opportunity to see a bush town of some 2500 people.

I did not know a soul, but soon found some men anxious to become my friends. One of them was a life insurance agent. He went as far as offering me a drink, which was an unwise thing for him to do, as beer and whisky are deadly in this place. So I refused the offer and offended my new friend.

Another man came, and with a great amount of discretion tried to find out if I were as much of a New Chum as I looked. He asked me whether I did not want a nice little property, and before I could say 'No,' took out of his pocket a bundle of particulars. All were the best properties on the market; some were 'tip-top,' some were real 'snaps'. The conversation ended by the offer of another drink and another polite but firm refusal.

The town does not look very lively; I counted fifteen hotels, and wondered how they could exist, though the place has the reputation of suffering from thirst.

I saw one of the local identities, 'Kookaburra Jack,' a pure blackfellow, who came to shake hands with me. His dress was partly military and partly mufti. The general dinginess of the outfit made a good blend of the whole. He asked me for some tobacco and for 3d. He has been through forty years of civilisation; all he has learned from the white man is to drink whisky and eat skilly.

The buildings, except the Police Station, look rather flimsy and without any style. Verandahs are a great feature of the place. They must be a necessity, for every other verandah post supports a man. I saw a fair amount of men in the main street who seem to have no pressing work to do. They smoke and spit for hours at a time without getting tired of either.

This place has a Jockey Club, a Trotting Club, a Cricket and Football Club, and a Pigeon Shooting Club. There must be a lot of money about here, though it does not give you this impression at first.

I heard that this town is renowned in New South Wales for its inflammability. Last year there were twenty-three fires. The local fire brigade arrived too late on twenty-four occasions, the twenty-fourth being a false alarm. The people must have become fireproof, for they always escape unhurt. The only architect of the town is also agent of a fire insurance company; he is doing well, they say.

Bill has received a letter from England, on crested paper, and he showed it to us. The writing was lacking firmness, but showed here and there that Sir Charles was trying hard to forget he had been Charley. The style was not befitting the beautiful 'cream laid'. He asked how everybody was, what the season was like, and inquired about the dogs. His sudden change of situation has left him cool-headed; he has not forgotten his friends, and has sent a good cheque to them as a token of remembrance. There was a PS at the foot of the last page:

'I have to pay a cove 25s a week to prevent anybody from killing the rabbits on my estate! I am sick of rabbits, and am thinking about importing a poison cart.'

We are five men, not counting the cook, pushing 2500 wethers in front of us. It is slow progress, but we will get to our destination in five weeks. We find nice corners at night for the sheep; some yards of calico and three dogs chained at stakes makes the watch an easy matter. All the same, I feel my responsibility heavily and keep my watch conscientiously. So far we had fine weather, plenty of feed and water. I like the life very much, no doubt because it is novel to me. I wonder how I would enjoy it in the middle of summer or during wet weather?

Henry, in charge, is an old man who speaks little and seldom smiles, except to his dog. Rusty is indeed a marvellous animal, who understands the sign of his master's hand, and is always eager for work. When the sheep go too much one way or another, Rusty looks at Henry and Henry knows something is wrong. He makes a sign, the dog disappears, and without a bark brings the sheep back into their line.

Bob the blackfellow is a highly civilised Aboriginal. He wears a rolled gold watch chain, a nickel watch, and sports an embroidered silk handkerchief, which he values too much to use. Jim and Bill are two young fellows full of life and mischief. I believe I am the first New Chum they have seen at close quarters. They don't think much of the species. They have analysed me from head to foot, and nothing has escaped their quick eye. My sheath knife amuses them, but they often require it. The way I ride, the length of my stirrup leathers amuse them vastly. My ignorance on the subject of horses and horseracing makes them really think I am a little simple.

The cook does not know how to cook the mutton which was sheep twenty minutes before. His puddings are good, solid work, and his tea is strong. Taken all round, we are a fairly happy lot, and when the pipes are lit and our toes are near the big camp fire the night birds may hear some fine fairy tales if they care to. A lot of the yarns are made up for my sole benefit. I pretend to take it all in, for I always enjoy looking a bigger fool than I am in reality.

This morning being Sunday, and the rightful owner of a certain patch of very good feed not being about, we only were on the road for a few hours and camped. There was a rush for a kerosene bucket, the property of the cook. Jim was first, and proceeded to boil his clothes, after which Bill took his turn. Then came mine, so I boiled my clothes with the air of a man who has managed a steam laundry. I was not going to ask questions, but would have liked to know how long the boiling was to last. I was afraid to get my clothes either underdone or parboiled, but I believe I did it about right. The cook came for his bucket, so I had to hurry the operation.

Half an hour after I recognised the bucket, with its crooked handle, on the cook's fire. There was a leg of mutton boiling inside. Of course I know it was only pure imagination, but I did not enjoy the dinner that day.

This summer has been terrible. We are in March, and no sign of rain yet. The ground is bare, for the yellow dead grass is nearly gone. The sheep are dying all over the paddocks, and the crows are everywhere, full of life and hellish joy. A few hours after their death the poor sheep who are mere skeletons look enormous and fat. It seems like a grim joke. Many of them die too slowly, so the crows help them along and add to their long agony. Nature is the cruelest thing on earth. Animals, most of them, cannot live or thrive without killing each other, so that very life means destruction. Man destroys more still, not only to keep himself alive, but to get rich or to amuse himself.

Yesterday I saw a bullock bogged in the creek up to his belly. One of his eyes was gone. He was feebly defending the other against the crows. I could do nothing, so I turned my back and fled, and I swore a swear which never crossed my lips nor my mind before. All this useless suffering, this fiendish cruelty to poor brutes who can't defend themselves make a man ask, 'Why?'

Rain has come at last. I never knew before what rain meant. I never dreamt what beautiful sound drops can make on an iron roof, what delicious smell dust has when the first shower pits the powdered red earth. All has been transformed in a moment. The men, like children, let the heavy downpour wet them to the skin. Animals seem to breathe it like draughts of new life. The very cockatoos hang head down from the tops of the trees, their wings spread open so as to get every drop on their feathers, while they shriek with a delight that is quite human. The colour of the trees has changed, the leaves have lost their dusty green, and are now vivid and glistening. Their trunks and their limbs are shiny. The earth, which looked a leper half an hour ago, has now a new complexion. It is once more the mighty Mother ready to give life.

We had all for weeks looked vainly at the sky. We had put our hopes in the small clouds which came towards us and then disappeared. We saw signs of a change in the way fowls did their feathers, in the halo round the moon, in the hurry of the ants round their nests. We ceased to believe in any sign till we got drenched.

After a wet winter and a flood, shearing came round again, but did not last long. There were not many sheep to shear, and a lamb was a curiosity. The place was understocked, the grass plentiful, so we had an awful bush fire. No stock was lost, but miles of fencing were burnt.

I have been a little over two years in Australia; I have seen a drought, a flood, and a fire. An earthquake is the next thing I expect.

I was thinking about the smiling future when Mary Smith reminded me in a long letter that she was still alive and still waiting for me. I hate to keep people waiting; on the other hand the Mary Smith ghost is casting a dark shadow on my life. I had nearly forgotten her during the last few months, and now she is with me once more.

The six pages (on scented paper) tell me what six pages had told me before. Her promise to come to Australia in the near future was still holding. Her love for me was not dying.

I had taken the firm resolution not to answer the letter, but after thinking and thinking, the fear took me once more of seeing Mary Smith landed in Australia. Finally I decided to write the following in a fairly well-disguised writing:

'Karaboo Downs, NSW
'Madame, It was necessary to open your letter addressed to Mr George Bell in order to return it. Mr George Bell died of a sunstroke two months ago. Yours faithfully,

W. P. Carr.'

It took me a long time to choose a death; I thought of snakebite, thirst, and blackfellows' spears. The sunstroke is not quite so picturesque, but it still has a fair amount of *couleur locale.*

Alf, the boy or groom, is a busy body. He has to milk the cows, kill the station sheep, cut wood, go for the mail, keep the place tidy, and do some 'odd jobs.' He is always required; he is everywhere. I believe he is the only man on the place who does not enjoy wet weather, for he has to run after his cows in the slushy yards. He sometimes finds the variety of his duties an excuse for having a little rest. When he is wanted to clean the laundry copper he has an appointment with a stray calf in the horse paddock. He likes visitors, and does cheerfully the extra work, as he gets a tip now and then.

Alf is a bit queer, but is a hard worker. He does get into rows at times with the cook, for bringing him red gum for his fire or for leaving the boots upon the kitchen table. He talks to himself by the hour, talks to the sheep he is going to kill, and gives him some little encouragement. He talks to the one-eyed cow who tries to kick him.

Alf has one great weakness; he is very fond of eggs. Mrs Telford found that out at last, though she had strong suspicions before. Alf since last month has to clean the fowl house, and ever since some of the fowls have stopped laying. The eggs were getting scarcer. Mrs Telford went on watching. Yesterday she saw Alf coming from the direction of the fowlhouse; she called him. Her quick eye could not but notice that Alf's shirt front was bulging in a singular way. Her plan was made in a second. She told him to crawl under the verandah floor, for she thought the cat must have died under the smoking room. Alf hesitated, and was going to mention an appointment with the killing sheep, but Mrs Telford did not give him time.

Alf disappeared under the floor where there was barely room for him to crawl. Mrs Telford could not help laughing. She asked him if he saw anything, and as nothing could be seen, she told him to come out. Alf extracted himself with difficulty, and rubbed

49

his eyes full of dust and cobwebs. The fact that he was carrying a raw omelette on his bosom was evident.

The fowls have started laying once more.

Blessed be the mailman, who has ridden sixty miles and opened seventeen gates on the road to bring me these two letters—one from my father; the fine old gentleman has put a nice sum at my disposition for the purchase of a station, should I feel able to start on my own. Fancy being one's own boss—sending Bill round the One Tree Paddock, Jim along the creek, and, if it is a very hot day, having some writing to do in the office!

I know I have still a lot to learn, so I will get some more colonial experience before I brand my own sheep and my own bales.

The second letter is from Joe, the best of friends:

'Your fiancée has borne the news of your death like—a woman! Within two months after the sad tidings she has managed to get engaged, and what is more, married to B. S. Snip, Esq. You may safely come to life once more.

'B. S. Snip is very rich; his father owns a prosperous tomato sauce factory, one of the best brands on the market (ask your grocer for it, and beware of imitations).'

My dignity will not allow me to congratulate Mrs B. S. Snip on her latest acquisition.

The blessed mailman has gone back carrying in his bag a letter to my father and one to Joe.

ADVICE TO NEW CHUMS.

I consider I know enough by this time to give New Chums a few tips which may be useful:

1. Try to keep an angelic temper and a live imagination, for you will have to see jokes.

2. Don't be too sensitive, and don't take literally all you are told. You will be called at times all sorts of names except your own. You will be presented with adjectives you never met before. It is only their way of expressing themselves.

3. Remember how to hold your gun. Don't forget that a stockwhip and an axe are always loaded.

4. When you give them a hand in the sheep yards don't split the mob unless you can't help it. Don't light your pipe in front of the gate when they are trying to get 1500 wild wethers through it.

5. Don't pat horses on the nose when they are tied up to a post. It means as a rule a broken bridle and a lot more besides.

6. Learn the pedigree of Carbine by heart. It will help you a lot.

7. When you hear a snake yarn, multiply the breadth by the length and divide by ten. Same calculation applies to Murray cods.

8. Don't try to make them believe that we, too, have sunsets in Europe.

9. Don't dare to say that their Southern Cross is crooked.

10. Don't resent being called a New Chum. Captain Cook was a New Chum when he landed in Australia. Most of the best men in this country were New Chums—Ned Kelly is an exception; he was born in Australia.

SELECTED STORIES

HOW BILL LARKINS WENT TO THE PARIS EXHIBITION

Bill Larkins let his horse's bridle fall to the ground and went into the store. The boss, with the art of a grocer, was busily stacking on the shelves tins of jam decorated with brightly coloured labels. Hodson turned around as he heard the jingling spurs.

Bill wished him good day, got his orders for the day's work, then asked for half a pound of tobacco. The boss, armed with a tomahawk, chopped off two wads of black derby from the contents of a small wooden chest with the top knocked off it and handed them to the man. Bill put one of them in his pocket and started attacking the other one with his knife as he went out of the store.

He already had one foot in the stirrup when he was called back.

'Bill,' said the boss, 'a letter for you; hang on, I almost forgot it.'

Bill spelled out the address on the envelope which he held clumsily, then opened it like a man who gets two letters a year.

It was a list of the winning numbers from Tattersall's lottery, which had been drawn after the Sydney Grand National Steeple Chase. Knowing his usual luck, he started to go through it without conviction:

1st prize, 9003 . . . £6,000 sterling
2nd prize, 3727 . . . £5,000 sterling
3rd prize, 1490 . . . £3,000 sterling

He went no further: 1490 was his number. He counted the zeros very carefully—it really was £3,000 sterling that he had won! His leg trembled when he got into the saddle; the horse wondered why he had deserved those two jabs of the spurs when they started; and Tim, the collie, followed him at a respectful distance, keeping an eye on his master.

Bill, who usually sat on his mount like a circus monkey, with his calves clinging to the animal's flanks and his back arched by the long galloping strides, had suddenly taken on the look of a conqueror. With his felt hat over his ear, his body straight and his legs stretched out to the full length of the stirrups, he blew defiant puffs of smoke at the blue sky. That morning the paddocks appeared charming to him, the eucalyptuses had a greenness about them which he had never noticed before. He rode mechanically along the fences. The fence-posts lined up monotonously as far as the eye could see, bearing six strands of wire which stretched out in a maddening infinite perspective.

When he passed close to the 1,500 four-tooth ewes (two and a half years old) which were coming back from the river escorted by their frisky lambs, Tim, his ears folded back and his tail wagging eagerly, looked at his master as if to ask whether he was needed.

But Bill was far away from his sheep. £3,000! he thought for the fifteenth time . . . Once again he pulled the piece of paper from his pocket: Number 1490: £3,000 sterling.

Lulled by the rapid pace of the horse, Bill could hear in the creaking of the saddle a music that transported him.

What would he do with this money? For six years now he had been regularly sending off his pound note to Tattersall's; each time he had got back a receipt and a list which invariably ignored the number of his ticket. He had often enough made up plans in anticipation of a possible fortune; now that the luck had come through he found that the plans he made and remade were not satisfactory.

He was just starting to make up a new set when the horse took a sideways step which brought him out of his daydreaming. In front of him a dead ewe lay in the grass; recently dead, for the crows had not yet touched it. He dismounted, took out his knife and began to carve up the animal. The speed with which he skinned the ewe was a good indication that this was not his first go at it; he hung out the skin on the fence wire and continued

56

on his solitary ride through the paddocks. Larkins was the type you often meet in the Australian bush: of medium size, solid build, but with almost frail legs, ending in dainty feet, made for the stirrup and not for walking; the face is small and the blue eyes which animate it have the depth and penetration of sailors' eyes used to looking into the far distance.

His earliest childhood companions had been tame lambs which owed to their condition of rescued orphans the right to wear their tail intact and the privilege of roaming at will around the house, indiscriminately munching on the cabbages in the tiny garden or the linen drying in the sun.

As soon as the bush school had finished teaching him its sketchy lessons, which scarcely overloaded his young brain, he had begun working in the sheds at shearing time. Proud of the ten shillings he earned each week, and feeling all the importance of his title and functions as tarboy, he had generously tarred up the wounds of sheep injured by clumsy shearers. Later on, he had bellowed in the yards amidst 2,000 agitated creatures which five men carrying on like demons and as many barking dogs could not drive from one enclosure into another. Covered in blood from head to foot, his hand weary and blistered from the instrument, he had nicked the ears of 2,700 lambs in one day. In the end, he had gradually learned all the tricks of the trade and had become a perfect Australian sheep man. He got to know the animals, took an interest in them and treated them with kindness as if they belonged to him.

By dint of living among sheep, Bill seemed to have borrowed something from them. His hooked nose, his thick, curly hair gave him a striking resemblance to a merino ram; if need be, he could imitate to perfection the deep-throated bleating of the ewe or the nasal whine of the lamb; moreover, his clothes always smelled like greasy wool.

His dog Tim, who never left him and backed him up on all his jobs, was probably the only creature he loved in the world; he was proud of him, and rightly so, telling anyone who would listen how Kelpie, Tim's father, had won first prize in the Sydney sheepdog trials.

So Bill was living happily and quietly in a world bounded by the fences of Barinda station when £3,000 suddenly shattered his peaceful existence.

He sent off his ticket number 1490 to Tasmania, to Hobart, where the agency, driven out of the other Australian colonies, had taken refuge; one week later, sure enough, he received a cheque to the value of £3,000 sterling.

He hadn't yet been able to make up his mind as to the use of this money; it never entered his thoughts to invest it in any way; the difficulty was to know how to spend it.

One morning he entrusted his dog to Jimmy, who, like himself, worked at Barinda, and rode off to the nearest railway station. He had decided to go to Sydney, which he had never seen; he would lead the grand life there, for he was suddenly feeling a thirst for that unknown luxury which money alone can give.

He arrived in the small town of Forbes after a ride of thirty miles and went straight to the bank, one of the few important buildings in the place. He tied up his horse to the post planted in front of the establishment and pushed open the glass door. The young man in shirt sleeves behind the counter, who was reading the report of the latest races in Sydney, consented to leave off his reading for a moment and raised his head, then greeted Bill Larkins with a sharp 'Good day' which meant: 'What do you want?'

Bill took out of his pocket a fourpenny notebook, all dirty and scribbled over, extracted the cheque and handed it to the employee. The latter took the piece of paper between his index and middle fingers, but could no longer maintain his nonchalant air when he read the amount.

'Yes, that's right, 3,000 pounds,' said Larkins, glad to be able to astound the young man with the enormous starched collar. And he pushed across the counter the list of lottery numbers together with the letter which accompanied the cheque.

The teller took all this, went to consult the manager, then came back and asked:

'In gold or in notes?'

'In notes,' said Bill, as if such a question was addressed to him every day of his life.

With his hand on the side of his chest which was swollen with banknotes, Larkins left the bank; the young man, who had quite forgotten his newspaper, followed him with his eyes.

The train left in an hour. Bill just had time to leave his horse with a publican he knew, and get something to eat.

In the first-class (smoking) compartment, the two travelling salesmen, already set up to play their game of whist, thought for a moment that the man in the soft hat and moleskin trousers had got into the wrong carriage; but the confident manner with which Bill settled himself into one corner left these gentlemen with some food for thought.

When night came, each man arranged himself as best he could to sleep, at the same time grumbling about the slow progress of the train which kept stopping at tiny stations lost in the plain, and whose baroque and complicated names might have raised a smile in other circumstances.

The next morning, about six o'clock, Bill alighted at Sydney and refused to take a cab, preferring to stretch his legs. He had found out in advance which was the best hotel, and good bushman that he was, easily found the Australia, where he arrived with his hands in his pockets.

The doorman, seeing the somewhat larrikinish cut of his clothes and the scantiness of his baggage, at first refused to give him a room; however, when Bill offered to pay in advance, he took him over to the desk where he was given a key.

After a breakfast such as he had never dreamed of, Bill walked down George Street where the shops were beginning to open. He went into one of them, found a grey suit which looked marvellous on him, according to the gentleman who served him; acquired some white shirts and some starched collars, things new to him; bought almost everything the salesman proposed, and emerged transformed after giving his address so that they could send him a new trunk filled with a complete new wardrobe.

Then began for Bill a delightful existence: races, evenings at the theatre, trips to Manly, he refused himself nothing. The lunches and dinners in the grand dining room of the Australia were first class; but the moment he was shown to a seat by a waiter in a dinner suit, and the moment he left it, were agony. Gentlemen and well-dressed ladies would watch him weaving his way among the small tables, and almost feeling giddy, Bill would put one hand on his hip and curl his moustache with the other hand in what he thought was a jaunty manner, and so as to put up what he hoped was a good front. In spite of that, he felt proud to be able to eat the same food as the rich squatters and the big mine owners.

Downstairs in the main vestibule of the hotel, travellers came and went; piles of trunks were being brought in and out at every moment. Bill amused himself reading the labels which covered this luggage; there were all sorts of them, in all colours, from all countries, and the bushman dreamed of all of these faraway places which he had often heard spoken of, but which only added up in his mind to a confused mass of peculiar countries and different races which he invariably called Negroes or half-bloods so long as they were not Anglo-Saxon.

Everybody seemed to be going off to Paris for the Exhibition; the newspapers were full of descriptions and photographs of the celebrations in the French capital; all the boats set sail full of tourists who wanted to see the Exhibition and spend their money in this city which attracted them like a beautiful woman.

While taking a stroll one morning, Bill found himself at Circular Quay; a P&O ship was just leaving from a wharf jammed with people sending their farewells to the passengers who were crowding the ship's deck. Larkins had never seen such a thing: and the majesty of the vessel slowly moving away, hailed by the shouting masses, thrilled him and suddenly gave him a mad desire to travel.

His mind was resolved: he too would go to Paris to see the Exhibition.

He went straight to the offices of a shipping company. All

60

the cabins had been long since reserved on the next two boats. He tried another company, but the answer was the same; at last, at the third one, luck came to his aid; a man had just died of the plague and the bunk he had booked was now free. Bill came out with a first-class ticket for Marseilles and Paris. The boat left in three days.

Although the first-class table was not exclusively made up of 'ladies' and 'gentlemen', Larkins did not feel any less ill at ease on the first night amidst all these people in evening dress. The menu which was passed to him listed dishes whose names, incomprehensible to him, ill concealed an English-style cuisine. He quickly singled himself out by his skill at eating peas and mashed potato with his knife. The place which was reserved for him provided very restricted room for his elbows when he was cutting his meat. His large work-scarred hands, with their broken and inadequately scrubbed nails, clashed with the white linen. On his left, the lady of mature years whose angular face was surmounted by a small lace bonnet did not seem very much inclined to conversation; so Bill contented himself with passing her the salt and water, of which the lady consumed a formidable amount. On his right, the plump, ruddy gentleman seemed more sociable. He had 'done' all the Australian colonies. He had endowed these fortunate regions with 763 American phonographs, latest model. He had had all sorts of curious adventures, and he didn't have to be asked twice to recount them at length.

Bill didn't take long to realise that he had strayed into a social milieu that was not really his. The ladies, both young and old, adopted unapproachable, distant airs, and the gentlemen, for the most part, had conversations which were of no interest to him.

In the smoking room, he would light up a cigar more to show that he could afford a Henry Clay rather than for the pleasure; for as soon as he had finished it, he would fill a pipe with derby; and the men who were playing poker at the nearest table would turn round to look at him at the first puff, sniffing the air in an unfriendly fashion.

He never really adapted to life on board. The weather was superb, the cabins luxurious; but the hours were long between meals for a man who, like Bill, was used to an active life. The ship's library was certainly well stocked; but the books had a forbidding air about them, all bound in dark green, and with uninviting titles. He loved a good horseracing story, such as Hawley Smart writes and which can be found everywhere in Australia; or else those tall stories of Mexican cowboys, Californian miners, or bushrangers, which abound in the bush huts, proudly bearing on their sensational cover illustration the glorious grime of long periods of service.

Larkins soon found the conversation of the stewards, cooks and sailors much more to his taste, then little by little he frequented the third-class deck, delighted to find himself in more familiar territory; there everyone smoked derby; you could spit in peace without fear of offending the delicate sensibility of a ship's officer. On the beautiful starry nights, while the first-class passengers looked as though they were bored stiff in the glow of their electric light, there would be dancing in the bows on the third-class deck; the stewards and the sailors would set to with their comical or sentimental songs, and everybody would join in the chorus accompanied by the accordion.

Bill soon became a favourite; they found him 'not stand-offish'; and then he would shout whiskies and cigars with the free and easy manner of a lord. The ladies declared he was a 'jolly fellow', and he was very popular on dance nights. It was not long before Mary Ann Smith made her girlfriends jealous, and the gossips went to work to vary the monotony of the voyage a little.

Mary Ann Smith was a young woman who had had a position as maid with a Sydney family and who was going home to London to rejoin her parents and live with them. She claimed however that she had been a schoolteacher, and backed up this small lie with manners that she had copied imperfectly; but the 'h's' of her mother tongue, which she dropped or sounded at random, betrayed her somewhat sketchy education.

But Larkins thought she was very nice and quickly fell for

Mary Ann's charms; long were their talks on the calm nights, both of them leaning on the ship's rail, watching the water rushing past the side of the ship, lit up by the cabin portholes. The sheep man, who only turned up in first class at meal times, would always go up to the bows with his pockets full of dessert to be greeted by Mary Ann with pleasure.

At Colombo, where the ship stopped for a day to take on coal, Bill took his new lady friend ashore. Travelling in rickshaws pulled by the Ceylonese, they went to Lavinia, admiring the beauties of nature and eating exotic fruits which they peeled clumsily.

Surrounded by this earthly paradise, Bill felt himself transported and his heart grew tender. While he was watching the sea spending itself on the palm-fringed shore, sitting next to Mary Ann and drinking an iced lemon squash, Bill posed an apparently embarrassing question to the young lady, for she blushed and stammered that it was 'a bit sudden'. Nevertheless, the answer was not too long in coming. Far from the noisy tourists, Bill led behind a clump of palm trees the woman who had just become his fiancée, and there he gave her their first kiss.

Coming back into town, Bill took Mary Ann into one of the numerous jeweller's shops in the arcades, and let her choose a gold ring bearing a precious stone, and a silver belt.

Back on board, big plans were made; Bill would have liked to find a cabin for his fiancée in first or second class. But all the places were taken. He proposed to accompany her to London, where the wedding would be held, then both would go to Paris for their honeymoon.

From then on Bill stuffed even more dessert into his pockets, and the days passed swiftly for the two lovers. They sailed through Aden, then Suez.

At Port Said they had several hours to go ashore; Mary Ann, suffering from the heat, preferred to remain on board, and Bill disembarked alone. He strolled through the town where the filth and vices of the four corners of the world were gathered together and prospering; he bought some Egyptian cigarettes, and a dark-skinned man took him to a gaming-house. Around a roulette table he found a cluster of people watching their stakes on the red or the black; he pushed his way through and his gambler's instinct could not resist. After half an hour, weary of losing, he came out, giving the Arab boy who was waiting for him a silver coin.

As he went back towards the quay, along which the donkey-drivers and pedlars eked out a terrible living, Bill went into a bazaar where they sold all sorts of exotic goods, most of which had been given their oriental trademark in Paris, Birmingham or Berlin. He bargained for a crescent-shaped brooch and prepared to pay for it when the obsequious merchant finally consented to lower his price by two-thirds.

He put his hand in his pocket . . . the wallet containing all his money had disappeared.

He ran back to the casino like a madman; the other passengers were hastily leaving it, for the strident whistle of the ship was sounding. He had to go back on board, his pockets empty, clutching his two cartons of cigarettes under his arm.

In the impossible hope of finding his money, Bill searched every corner of his cabin, emptied his trunk and his suitcases on the carpet, but all without success. While he frantically looked through his clothes that he hadn't even worn yet, he calculated that he had one pound, seven shillings and sixpence left.

He immediately thought of Mary Ann. What would happen to all their plans?

After dinner, he descended the narrow, low-ceilinged stairs that led to third class and found Miss Smith waiting for him. When he took out of his pockets an apple, an orange and some almonds, Mary Ann seemed to ask him if he hadn't bought something for her in Port Said: he gave the excuse that he hadn't seen anything ashore worth looking at.

This answer didn't satisfy the fiancée, who pouted and remained silent; Bill was grateful to her for not prolonging their meeting that evening.

The several days of the crossing from Port Said to Marseilles were no fun for poor Bill, and his loss seemed even more cruel in the luxurious surroundings of first class.

Mary Ann continued to make plans, describing to Bill the beauties of London, the Thames, the Crystal Palace and Madame Tussaud's; the man could only reply to all that with a few words that burnt his lips and broke his heart. She noticed that her 'darling' was not his old self and asked him the reason. Bill, who wanted to get it over and done with as soon as possible, told the whole story.

Mary Ann wept, then grew angry at having been deceived, finally threatening the man to drag him before the courts for breach of promise. The encounter was a stormy one; Bill went back to his cabin and slept very badly.

The next day he went to find the chief officer, explained his case in detail, and asked how he could get back to Australia.

The officer replied that there was only one way: to work for his passage from Marseilles to London and from London to Sydney.

Bill thanked him, saying that he would think it over.

One morning the stopping of the propeller woke him up; he dressed hastily and went up on deck. The port of Marseilles and the violet mountains which framed it left him cold; he waited for the chief officer to come down from the bridge in order to tell him his decision. The officer promised him a passage and made an appointment with him for that evening.

Then Bill thought of getting rid of all his rich man's gear, his trunks and suitcases, still brand new, and his now useless gentleman's wardrobe. He was directed to a man who spoke broken English and who, upon examination of the luggage and its contents, consented to make a deal by offering him ten pounds; it was approximately a quarter of the value, but faced with necessity, Bill pocketed the sum offered.

That evening, when they had left behind the lights of Marseilles in the wake of the ship, when Mary Ann caught sight of Bill in an apron, peeling potatoes at the galley door, she forgot about dragging the unfaithful ex-fiancé before the court.

They sailed past Gibraltar and up the coast of Spain; the sea

65

turned rough in the Bay of Biscay; there was a storm. Bill, who up to that time had never known really bad weather, and who had not experienced seasickness, went through hell for two days and two nights.

Tossed from right to left in his narrow bunk, situated just above the propeller, his wandering thoughts recalled his former cabin and the comfort of first class, his fortune so soon vanished and that short-lived idyll.

As far as London, the sea was in such a state that the passengers hardly ever showed themselves on deck; as soon as they entered the Thames, yellow faces or faces pale as ghosts emerged one by one into the light.

He was busy pumping water into a tub when he saw Mary Ann loaded up with her bags, getting ready to disembark. She walkd close by him without deigning to look at him; this indifference hurt him, then gradually consoled him for the loss of his fiancée.

The return voyage to Australia seemed long, for he was sick more than once. At last, one evening, the ship sailed through the Heads and entered Sydney's marvellous harbour.

Bill is now back at Barinda, as before; there he is reunited with Tim, his horse and his sheep; and when he slowly drives a flock over the paddocks, he breathes in with pleasure the smells of greasy wool and trampled grass that the animals leave behind in their passing. One by one he runs through a string of memories which are now only so many regrets.

In the evenings, when pipes are lit in the hut and men gather round the fireplace, he consoles himself a little by telling Jimmy, Ned and the others how he spent £25,000 sterling in a fortnight at the Paris Exhibition! They listen to him in amazement, envy him and call him 'lucky bastard'.

Five minutes later he is curled up under his old blanket; he thinks of Mary Ann, drifts slowly off to sleep, and dreams that he is tossing about on the Bay of Biscay.

(First published in *A l'autre bout du monde,* 1905)

CHARLEY

About fifteen miles from the station on one of the bends in the river you'll find the camp of old Charley the rabbiter. Under the tall Australian gums, which throw shade only from their trunks, the little canvas tent is pitched two steps from a smoking heap of white cinders. A square of warped bark mounted on four posts serves as a table and holds some kitchen utensils, in the middle of which sits the bushman's traditional billy and its inseparable tin mug.

Between two trees and at head height stretch wires on which hang two or three hundred rabbit skins and as many scalps or pairs of ears. When the master is home thirty skinny dogs, of all colours and sizes but of no special breed, welcome you with their furious barking.

Each morning, after having made his tea and burned a chop or two on a homemade wire grill, Charley unties the howling pack and takes off on his horse across the arid country, sometimes without seeing water again the whole day.

Rabbits run everywhere, white, black, red and grey. The starved pack separates into groups; you can hear the cries of the victims struggling in the dogs' throats.

Charley's raucous shouts, and a few swearwords which embellish them, are the only thing to stop the dogs in their scramble. The trapper dismounts and, with his knife in his hand, cuts up the dead rabbits quick as a wink and puts the skins in his bag, while the dogs fight over the bleeding carcases, each one tugging in his own direction.

So the hunt continues; but the sun soon becomes overpowering; the dogs walk in line, tongues hanging out, indifferent to the rabbits which criss-cross the plain in every direction.

They make their way slowly back to camp and the sun is

low when the old man arrives back under the river gums. The skins and scalps are hung and join the garland of trophies which attract black swarms of buzzing flies. The dogs throw themselves into the river and swim alongside the bank, all the time drinking the water for dear life. Charley comes down in his turn, performs his ablutions, and stretched out on his belly, face down in the water, he revels in the refreshment. Then he fills the billy, which is soon singing on the rekindled fire.

At nightfall the dogs are chained up; the laughing jackasses snigger their first notes. Seated on a sheepskin, the old man smokes his pipe, his eyes lost in the glowing fire which lights up the surrounding trees.

Each day follows identically upon the other in Charley's life. He goes for weeks, even months, without seeing a soul. From time to time he goes off to the station to take in his skins, replenish his rations and tobacco, and to find out the date, for he has lost all sense of time.

Every six months he sends several bundles of skins to Sydney and is paid well for them: and at the station he gets sixpence a scalp. Time was when they were worth fifteen shillings apiece! Lucky members of the profession used to run a carriage drawn by horses wearing silver rabbits on all parts of the harness.

In the bush, if you earn money you don't save it, and Charley, like the others, would go through in four days the cheque that had taken six months' hard work to earn.

The closest supply of whisky was only forty-five miles from the camp. The old man would set off one fine morning with a piece of paper worth £160 or £170 in his trouser pocket. That same evening he would arrive at the place of his dreams and drink for three solid days, then on the fourth, without a penny left, he would get back in the saddle, his head fuddled, his face bruised in some fall or a fight and quite horrible to see, framed by his white beard. Arriving back at the camp more by good luck than good management, Charley would take off again across country the very next day, preceded by his dogs which hadn't eaten for six days.

One morning, on going up to the house, Charley found an envelope addressed to him from Sydney and containing a cheque for £200. The previous season had been good for rabbit-catchers: no rain for five months, sheep dying like flies and rabbits able to be caught by hand. The pelts weren't heavy, but there were so many of them!

Charley whipped back to his camp without losing any time. He put away safely in his tent the little calico bags which held sugar, salt and flour; he made sure the dogs were all chained and remounted to return to the pub.

The road was long and monotonous; no trees were visible once you left the river; the plain was blinding under the sun and not one blade of grass poked out of the bare, cracked ground. Not a breath, not a sound; the sad countryside seemed to dance, seen through the steam rising from the ground. The few stray sheep in this emptiness looked like cattle, under the influence of this mirage, and the rabbit burrows like veritable hills.

The rider, with his hat pulled down over his eyes, swayed to the rhythm of his old horse; sometimes the beast sank up to the hocks on all four legs into a hole undermined by the damned rodents. Charley would stand up for a moment, relight his pipe and muse over the thirst-quenchers to be enjoyed on arrival after forty-five miles in the fierce sun with 104 degrees in the shade.

At sunset the pub appeared at last, making a tin-toy profile on the red horizon with its corrugated iron roof and tiny verandah.

Charley quickly dismounted, unsaddled his horse who, once free, shook himself, then having rolled two or three times in the dust, went over to a small pond which shimmered a few yards away.

Three swaggies, sitting on their heels and smoking in the shade of the verandah, quickly responded to Charley's signal and followed him into the bar which, from one end of the year to the other, gave off a rancid smell of local beer and poor quality whisky. The hotel-keeper welcomed his old friend with a smile on his lips, knowing that the rabbiter's visit always meant another £100 or so in his honest pocket.

The glasses were lined up on the wooden counter and were filled and emptied in turn with perfect regularity.

Charley, his thirst quenched after the fourth whisky and soda, went to the store close by and made some purchases.

Architecturally, the store was just a replica of the pub; but a bit of everything was sold there, from saddles and tobacco to clothing and jam. The old man came out after a quarter of an hour wearing brand new things from top to toe, and proudly smoking a new meerschaum pipe with a heavy silver mounting.

At dinnertime, heavy waggons laden with merchandise pulled up in front of the hotel verandah. The men, at Charley's invitation, hurried to unhitch their beasts, and after one or two rounds everyone went to the table.

The meal was jolly and all enjoyed the corned beef accompanied by canned potatoes. A well-known champagne had somehow ended up in this desert country; the one and only case was called upon. Corks popped, they drank from pannikins, and these men who lived for months with tea or water as their only drink now drank the champagne in great gulps.

Charley held out rather well; but there came the time when he had to be carried to his bed, where he slept like a log right through until late the next morning.

He woke up dazed and began with a glass of brandy to pull himself together; he pulled out of his pocket a wad of banknotes, and throwing them on the counter, he told the landlord: 'Let me know when I've gone through it.' There was £160 in it.

The same performance of the day before recommenced; they drank the whole day, the hotel was open to all comers, and the drinks were on Charley. That same evening he slept very soundly under the verandah; another day passed, and on the morning of the fourth the landlord told him he'd come to the end of his bankroll.

His horse was led up, he was hoisted into the saddle, and beast and rider took off about noon on their long and lonely journey.

Charley, his arms dangling, his head lolling on his shoulders, left it to his mount to get him home.

About a mile from the camp the river formed a lagoon whose muddy edges and bottom were known and dreaded by all the locals and which had been given the name 'the Glue Pot'. There was actually only one place where you could cross it with impunity; you would find sheep in groups of five or six stuck up to their bellies at the water's edge and eaten alive by the voracious crows when their death throes were considered too slow. At low water you could see the carcases of cattle and horses which had perished trying to drink at this treacherous waterhole.

Charley scarcely gave a thought to the lagoon when towards midnight his horse stopped near its banks and tested the ground before attempting to drink. With neck out and pursed lips the animal sipped at the water; but when his feet suddenly started to sink under him, he jerked back, pulled himself out and turned quite around.

The old man woke up from his doze and looked around him.

The lagoon appeared to him to shine in the moonlight, smooth as a silver platter. He broke off a stout branch within reach, stripped it of its leaves, and turning the horse's head, he forced it to walk on.

Once in the water, the horse stopped and drank in deep draughts; Charley watched it stupidly, staring at the bright circles spreading out over the tranquil lake to go and lose themselves on the other side.

Once its thirst was quenched the horse lifted its head; Charley gave him two sharp jabs with his spurs. The poor mount strained with all four limbs, pulled itself free with difficulty, walked a few steps then stopped, brushing up against a large tree which had grown in the middle of the lagoon.

The old chap now had his feet in the water and the spurs were becoming useless. He broke the branch he was holding on the animal's rump; it made a last effort, plunged in further, then, resignedly, stood stock still, firmly stuck in the mud.

Charley swore and shouted, threw his stick away, thus rousing the white ibises which flew off in fright. Suddenly, he remembered he had a bottle in his pocket; he pulled it out, looked at its contents in the light of the moon, and drank half. He filled his pipe, lit it and smoked as if nothing was wrong. But soon his head dropped, and his body stretched out along the neck of the immobile horse. The pipe fell into the water and disappeared, sizzling. The man fell asleep.

Awkwardly seated in his saddle, he leaned bit by bit to the left; his right foot came out of the stirrup, and suddenly his whole body fell into the lagoon. The water bubbled for a moment, then became muddy; a hand black with mud appeared for a second at the surface, then the lake became calm again.

Two months later, a rider passing by Charley's camp found thirty dead dogs, still chained, and picked clean by the crows.

Further on, in the middle of the low waters of the 'Glue Pot', he saw a fully saddled horse standing propped against a tree; its white bones were beginning to show through its leathery, wizened skin. At the end of the summer the lagoon, completely dried up, revealed Charley's body—embedded like a fossil in the cracked dried clay.

(First published in *A l'autre bout du monde*, 1905.
Translated by Margaret Whitlam)

JIM AND JACK

Over the banks of an Australian river, in New South Wales, rise the white roofs of the station of Bingarella. Clear in the summertime, the waters run low between their jagged banks; rising from their bed in the wintertime, they are muddy and repeatedly carry off great tree trunks in their fast-flowing eddies and currents.

On either side eucalypts have grown, strong from the cool moistness which feeds their roots. Quite tall and powerful at their advanced age, they saw long ago the many fires of the black encampments at a time when the kangaroos wandered as masters over the plain, accompanied by the more timid emus.

Some of these gums still bore the traces of the stone axe-blades, and with the years these wounds have opened out as the scars formed over them.

Bingarella carried about 80,000 sheep, as well as the 800 cattle and horses which roamed over it half wild.

Every morning at daybreak the men got into the saddle and set off in all directions, some to check the condition of the fences separating the many paddocks, others to round up the cattle or count the sheep.

In the evening, when the sun on the rim of the plain traced giraffe-like shadows before the eyes of horsemen weary after eight hours in the saddle, the station, which had been deserted all day, came back to life. Once dinner was over, a piano could be heard in the boss's cottage, and 'The Virgin's Prayer' blended in the mild night air with a music hall ditty sung by the men on the verandah of their hut, accompanying themselves on the accordion. These men, about ten in number, had mostly been born in the colonies, dark-haired ones of Irish stock and fair ones with Scottish blood. They all seemed lean and wiry, tanned under their soft felt hats which they only took off at the moment of going to bed, and good horsemen, ready to take on the buckjumpers and having some experience of their treacherous leaps and unexpected sidesteps.

Jim and Jack, who had been at the station the longest, and who were also the hardiest workers, had long since formed a close friendship (or as they would have said, were great mates).

For several weeks now, they had been saddling up fresh horses as soon as they had shaken out the last dregs of their pannikin of tea onto the hut floor. Forgetting the forty or fifty miles they had ridden during the day under the oblique sun over the bare plain, they would ride off together into the dark on their way to say goodnight to the selector's daughter.

The two mates had a soft spot for Maggie, but their rivalry had not yet appeared real to them, and had in no way affected their almost brotherly bond.

Old Bill, who owned five or six hundred acres on the Bingarella run, greeted them every night with a friendly 'Hullo!' Maggie would tidy up inside, while the three men, sucking on their pipes, chatted at the door of the bark hut.

The selector would go inside when Maggie appeared and joined in the conversation. He didn't like, he said, to interfere in young people's affairs; but in reality he couldn't wait to finish a novel whose grubby cover indicated the large number of readers who had already devoured it. He would light a rag wick stuck in some sheep's lard and would take up his story just as the hero 'Big John' was up to his eighth Indian.

Outside, the conversation would go on till fairly late, and when the Southern Cross began to set, the two mates would leap into the saddle and ride back to the station, shaken by the rhythmical galloping of their horses.

One night, Maggie, sitting between Jim and Jack, was chattering on like all those of her species; the two men listened, noses in the air.

Suddenly a star described a curve in the sky and shot off

like some huge rocket. Without moving her head, Maggie asked: 'Did you make a wish?'

They didn't answer; she repeated the question. They turned their heads, looked at each other and said together: 'No, did you?'

'I saw the star too late,' Maggie said simply.

This slight incident, of no apparent importance, made a deep impression on the minds of the two mates; that night, they suddenly saw more clearly that they loved the same woman, and they returned to the station in a reflective mood.

As they said goodnight, they agreed that they would declare themselves to Maggie the next day and ask her to make her choice.

But the following night, the young woman candidly answered them by saying that she liked them both as friends, and nothing more.

. Jim and Jack were not satisfied and refused to believe Maggie's words. The situation seemed no less intolerable to them and they wanted to put an end to it, but put an end to it without ceasing to be mates.

One morning the boss called them both to give them a job which they alone on the station could do properly. He wanted them to chop down two enormous gum trees which went in the district under the name of 'the twins'. They had both grown up a few yards from each other, both equally strong, and tall and slim as masts.

Armed with their American axes, Jim and Jack mounted their horses to go and cut down the trees.

'Jack,' said the other man suddenly, 'I'm going to make you a proposition: the twins are equal in size and height, we are equal in strength, and our axes are good. We will choose our tree by lot, we will begin together, and the last one to chop down his tree will stand aside for the other . . . Do you understand?'

'All right!' said Jack, like a true Australian who loves a contest, whatever it is.

Arriving at the foot of the twins, the men jumped down and let their horses wander off, reins dragging, as was the local custom.

Lots were drawn, each man examined his axe, caressed the cutting edge with his thumb, and sized up his tree.

'Who'll give the signal?' said Jim.

Jack looked up; on the upper branches of a nearby tree a noisy cockatoo had just landed, angrily raising his yellow crest.

'When he takes off,' said Jack, 'we'll begin.'

Their eyes were fixed on the bird. After a long half-minute he took flight: the axes fell as one onto the thick bark.

The shining blades fell with a dull sound, throwing off enormous woodchips; they flew up again moist, covered with the red sticky gum that looked like blood.

A big wedge had already been cut out on the side of each tree, quite cleanly, and as neat as if it had been cut from a melon. Together Jim and Jack attacked the other portion of the trunk; up to now their chances were equal. Once again pieces of bark as big as a hand flew off, then the wound opened, grew wider, and the heart appeared dark purple.

The two men streamed with sweat, but their bare arms rose and fell without pause; Jim and Jack were fighting for their lives. The twins' foliage began to tremble at the summit, shaken by the repeated blows. Only a thin section held up the trees now, a few more bites from the axe would give them the final blow.

Suddenly Jack's tree snapped, then leaning, seemed to hesitate for an instant. The leaves hissed in the air, and the giant fell with a crash, breaking in its fall the surrounding small trees. Its hollow branches, shelter for possums and galahs, shattered like glass, and pieces of them penetrated into the ground.

Jim had watched all this and went pale. He was one stroke of the axe behind, and he gave it. His tree fell, and while the gum seemed to be thrashing the air with its great arms, Jim threw himself under the collapsing trunk and disappeared beneath the inert mass.

Letting out an oath, Jack ran to the spot where his mate lay. His back broken under the wooden colossus, poor Jim was lying on his belly, face down in the grass and his arms stretched out before him.

Jack set to work to free the body, having to cut through the trunk in two places, and after an hour of heavy labour, he was able to contemplate the dead man's calm face.

Jack had witnessed the suicide, but to protect the memory of his mate, he gave out that it was an accident.

That same evening, at sunset, the boss and the men arrived on horseback from the station with a pick and shovel.

At the foot of the tree cut down by Jim they dug a hole. Jack wrapped his dead mate in a blanket, each man took a souvenir of the deceased, one his pipe, another his knife, and the body was slipped into its last resting place.

They all stood round the gaping hole, hat in hand. These rough men, used to swearing and blaspheming, listened to some verses from the Bible with their eyes downcast. The tears came unashamed, and with a lump in their throats, some for the first time perhaps, they thought of death in all its ugliness.

With the prayers over, the lumps of earth fell silently onto the grey woollen blanket, and when the dead man was left in peace, a kookaburra began to laugh on the top branch of a gum tree, no doubt surprised to see the twins laid out on the ground.

And that is why, at Bingarella, Maggie has stayed an old maid and Jack has lost his cheerfulness.

(First published in *A l'autre bout du monde*, 1905)

PICKY

As soon as she heard the horse pull up, Picky stopped teasing the young kangaroo which was poised on his long front paws and powerful tail, warding off like a well-trained boxer the feints and jabs she had been throwing at him for some time. The young black girl went and planted herself in front of her master, and while he unsaddled, she watched his every move with her wide open eyes. Her hands played in her short, thickly matted hair as she probed the ground with her bare feet whose toes instinctively sought to grab the stones lying within their reach.

'Hullo, Picky!' said Thompson. 'What do you say?'

'Good evening, master,' said the child, as if reciting a lesson.

She followed him onto the verandah, admiring his spurs which pleased her with their noise, and went in with him into the office, a small room cluttered with papers, bottles of medicine, whips, Winchesters and revolvers. The man sat down, stretched out his legs, and Picky, squatting, took off his spurs, leggings and boots, then put on his slippers for him.

'Well, Picky,' said the boss as he sugared the cup of tea which the Chinese cook had just brought in, 'what have they taught you today?'

The little girl flashed her white teeth in an inane smile, then looked at the floor on which she was drawing pictures with the rowel of a spur.

'Miss,' she replied at length in a telegraphic English in which the auxiliaries and the articles appeared at very rare intervals, 'Miss tell story big flood, big boat, many animals.'

And since the boss had understood that it was about the Flood and Noah's Ark, he showed interest and asked for details.

'Many animals,' she continued, 'horses, dogs, kangaroos, emus, possums, pelicans and then cockatoos; all in big boat . . . and then boss, lubras, piccaninnies, whole tribe.'

78

Thompson congratulated her on her memory and smiled as he thought of the efforts of imagination and patience that his daughter had had to make to get the story of Noah into that small native head.

He was going to ask her some more questions when someone came up, calling Picky as if for a reprimand. Miss Jane flew into the office, kissed her father and looked for the guilty one who was under the table.

'Picky,' she said, 'where are your stockings and shoes? Go and put them on immediately, quick!'

And Picky ran out, not without a look at the angry face of the daughter and the kindly air of the father.

Sitting on the verandah, the poor victim of civilisation began the operation of putting on her shoes, which was always a long and delicate one for her. She stood up at last, decorated with a pair of black stockings and elastic-sided boots, inside which her rebellious toes could still pretend to seek out stones.

Thompson, who ran the station of Taringa Downs situated in northern Queensland, had taken in eight years before an old gin accompanied by a little girl, whom one of the men had found half dead beside the creek. Old Mary, as she had been baptised, recounted how her tribe, accused of having speared to death several head of cattle, had been 'dispersed' by the police; and except for herself and Picky, the whole camp, eighteen men, women and children, had been killed by the troopers.

Miss Thompson had taken an interest in the fate of the fugitives; she had given the old woman a dress and a flowered hat (her father had pleased the woman more by offering her a pipe and some tobacco) and she had undertaken to bring up Picky so as to make her a Christian woman possessing the precious gifts of civilisation.

Thompson knew the natives, and had killed two or three out of necessity, yet he wasn't a cruel man. He didn't believe in turning the blacks white and barely concealed his scepticism in that regard; however, he let Jane go ahead, as she was religious by nature, like the mother she had lost ten years before. He often reminded her not to put too much of her heart and soul into Picky's education; for that task most often is a thankless one, and her young pupil might well, one day, like so many others of her kind, disappear never to come back again.

But Jane had faith in her mission. She belonged to several religious societies spread throughout the world which worked towards the noble aim of endowing savages with clothing for which they had no need, and of giving them religious instruction which, with a few rare exceptions, made them into hypocrites and not Christians. She subscribed to journals: *The Southern Cross, The Blacks' Friend,* the *Bulletin of the Aboriginal Advancement Society,* and corresponded with the central missions, reporting on her personal experience and on the successful fruits of her efforts with her pupil. Her simple soul which did not believe in evil was totally involved in this work of devotion and angelic patience. Besides, life for a young woman was poor in distractions on the stations in northern Queensland; communications were difficult, and it took four days' coach travel to reach a town of 300 and a post office. Visitors were rare and generally not very interesting for Jane; commission agents for the sale of sheep and cattle or commercial travellers in wholesale groceries were not her cup of tea.

Once a month, however, a short clergyman would arrive in his buggy, covered in dust or soaked to the skin, but always with a smiling, kindly air. The Reverend Smith was always warmly welcomed at Taringa Downs, and Jane, who admired his devotion and courage in his thankless task, would revel in making his stay at the station as pleasant as possible.

He would stay on the station for forty-eight hours, which he called his holiday; the rest of his time was spent driving along nameless tracks from one station to another, holding a small service, taking up his meagre and timid collection, then disappearing. At shearing time he would go from one shed to another, and in the evenings, surrounded by fifty or so shearers, coarse men who swore, blasphemed and drank whenever they had the chance, the Reverend Smith would deliver them a short sermon disguised in the form of a mild, friendly chat. These men who kept their pipes between their teeth and their hats on their heads from morning till night would remove their hats and stop smoking when the clean-shaven little clergyman appeared amongst them. They would all listen to him in silence; then they would put their sixpence or their shilling in the hat which went round.

Jane used to tell him about her pupil, of whom she expected so much, and Picky, who had put on her best clothes for the occasion and had pulled on her stockings with extraordinary care and energy, would recite her favourite lesson for the pastor, count up to seventy-five, making only two mistakes, and show how she could sew on a button using lots of thread. Jane would receive the Reverend Smith's compliments with barely concealed joy, and the two of them would excitedly discuss the child's future.

Seeing them occupied, Picky would sneak off to join Old Mary who, sitting at the door of her hut, would be packing a clay pipe, her toes stretched out in the sun.

Miss Jane and Mr Smith would certainly have been shocked to the depths of their feelings if they had seen their protégée crouched before the old woman's fire and sharing with her a goanna roasted in its skin, eating it with her bare teeth and without a fork!

One day, alas, a brand new white dress bore the traces of one of those unauthorised feasts, and Picky no longer got permission to go to the camp. Jane, helped by the clergyman, had on many occasions tried to convert the old gin, but she had always shown herself to be unshakeable in her narrow-mindedness, finding in her stumpy pipe and wads of tobacco the only satisfactory benefits of civilisation.

So they kept an eye on young Picky, fearing, as the Reverend Smith said, that Mary's influence might wither in her heart the precious buds from which they hoped for such fine fruits.

As the years passed, Picky made progress and showed an intelligence and memory which might not have been suspected to exist in her thick myall skull. She could now read the Bible that Miss Jane had given her and could say her daily prayers without mistakes. She had begun arithmetic, could sing 'There is a happy land' reasonably well, and could sew without pricking her monkey-like fingers too often.

But her spare time was spent putting into practice the lessons of Old Mary, whom she saw often in spite of everything. She had been given a doll one day, but this doll had a short life; for the gin had the brilliant idea, which Picky seized on eagerly, of opening its belly and putting it on the fire. The result surpassed all expectations of the experiment, and the two blacks anxiously watched the rubber body twisting and disappearing in a big flame and acrid smoke.

Picky preferred going off to chase lizards, making spears, or rubbing sticks to make fire as Mary had shown her. In the evening, when all were asleep at the station, Miss Jane's pupil would quietly leave her room and, barefoot, gliding along like a shadow, would cross through the garden to go and find Mary at her camp. The old woman was always busy with her witch's cooking, roasting some animal or other: a possum, a goanna, or even a snake she had caught.

Picky never refused a morsel of these choice dishes which she appreciated all the more because she never saw them on the dining room table; while the two women, their hands glistening with grease, carefully gnawed on their bones, the old lubra would tell the young black girl a thousand new things, more comprehensible and amusing than Miss Jane's things.

Picky had recited her story of the Flood and her Judgement of Solomon; but the old woman, pulling a horrible face, would say 'Bunkum!' and begin telling the fable of the Lizard and the Pink Cockatoo: Once there was a battle between the Lizard and the Pink Cockatoo; the reptile took a knife made from a flint set into a bone handle and made a cut into the bird's head. The result was that a crest appeared like a wood-shaving cut from the Cockatoo's skull, and the blood flowing down over its body and neck gave a pretty colour to its plumage. The Cockatoo avenged itself by throwing a large quantity of sharp-edged gravel onto the Lizard's back, causing the rough appearance of its skin.

Then, encouraged by the approval of her audience, which wanted more, she told the legend of the Kite and the Echidna: the Kite, who detested the Echidna, hurled at the poor beast a rain of spears which remained stuck all over its body; but as punishment, the bird was condemned to a life of eating raw flesh.

Mary would also describe, with many a grimace and gesture, the corroborees which she had witnessed in her tribe, the nocturnal dances around a large fire, in which the warriors daubed with white and red would dance to the music of strange songs accompanied by the sound of boomerangs struck together.

She told her about the 'death-bone' with which you could avenge yourself on an enemy at a distance, and the 'death-powder' which was put under the head of a sleeping rival. She explained how to make a man blind by pointing two possum's teeth at his eyes without his knowledge.

Picky, marvelling at all this, would creep back, trembling, to her little bedroom; then she would fall into a deep sleep during which pagan ceremonies mixed with stories from the Holy Bible would leave a strange confusion in her young mind.

Every day Thompson rode through the immense paddocks of Taringa Downs, and sometimes he had to camp at the other end of the run, fifty miles from the house. He had a flock of 100,000 sheep and 1,500 cattle to look after, as well as the artesian bores which watered the animals far from the river. He also had to keep an eye on his men, the stockmen, the boundary riders; in short, administer an area of land as big as a province in some European country.

Having noticed on several occasions the disappearance of a certain number of cattle whose tracks petered out on the other side of the river, Thompson wrote to the manager of Corella, his neighbour, asking him to send over a black who could track down the missing animals.

Corella didn't have a single white worker; they were all natives, inexpensive to keep and excellent stockmen. You could even find there a gin in moleskin trousers, flannel shirt and soft hat, who used to gallop over the paddocks and watch over the sheep. She was known all round the district and delighted the rare visitors. No doubt she didn't sit very nobly in her man's saddle; her naturally ugly profile was further spoiled by a horse's kick that would easily have killed two white men at a single blow; but on the other hand, she was the best stockman on the station, and at lambing time she was a real mother to the little lost ones that she saved from the greedy crows.

The manager of Corella was too fond of his horsewoman to let her go; but he sent over to Thompson a man named Billy, whom he recommended highly. He was a solidly built black who had once served for two years as a blacktracker in the mounted police. Just like all of his race, he could read the ground as we read a book; when he was with his tribe he could recognise from a footprint which of his relatives had passed by at that spot, and many a time he had amused himself by imitating with the impression of his fingers in the sand the tracks of the emu, the kangaroo or even the white man's shoe.

He had only one fault, added the manager of Corella in his letter to Thompson, he would get as drunk as . . . a white man. So Billy arrived one morning at Taringa and immediately went to work, in exchange for a pound of tobacco per week, food and clothing. Three days later he returned with the cattle he had found, and Thompson was delighted with his new acquisition.

Old Mary, having heard that there was a new black boy at the station, naturally wanted to see him: the first thing that stood out when she observed him going from the cookhouse to the stables was his walk; for he still kept his trooper's manner as if he was done up in his black tunic with silver buttons, his tight breeches tucked into long boots, and wearing his hat over his ear with the jaunty air of a military man.

Mary immediately pulled a face, in her usual way, then went over to have a talk. But Billy, who had become civilised some time ago, was beginning to despise his own colour and didn't respond to the gin's advances.

She, however, withdrew satisfied; for she had learned more than she hoped for: Billy had a large hole in his left ear.

The old lubra went into her hut, spoke to herself and gesticulated as she invoked twelve-year-old memories. She saw once again the camp suddenly invaded by the police and surrounded on all sides. She saw the men, caught unawares, hastily grabbing their spears, throwing some boomerangs while the women and the piccaninnies were running away screaming.

III

Having wandered away from the camp, and carrying her grand-daughter in a piece of bark, she had seen the troopers move up; but too late to give the alarm. Hidden in the bushes, she could hear the cries and the gunshots; cautiously raising her head, she saw a gin running away mad with fear, pursued by a black trooper who had quickly shot her down with a revolver at close range. The mounted trooper was coming over towards her when a spear went through his ear and the furious black turned to charge his aggressor.

Gradually silence returned, and as night fell she saw the glow of the burning humpies, then the whole plain seemed dead.

She waited for daylight to come out of her hiding place, frequently stifling the tears of the little one.

When the sun appeared, she quietly approached the camp, and amongst the corpses scattered in every position, she looked for some food for the child and for herself. She took away what she could carry, some nardoo seeds, a half-full possum-skin waterbag, and fled from this place of horror.

Billy, she had no doubts, was the blacktracker so determined on the evil carnage which had wiped out the tribe, and the years had not been able to remove the mark of the spear which had passed through his ear. Besides, the black man who puts on the police uniform becomes, by that very act, the enemy of his tribe as well as of others; and Mary naturally deduced that the man had to die.

But she, a lubra, according to the laws, did not have the right to kill; her only role was to look for food, to carry game and water. The desire for revenge was stronger than anything else; so she reflected on the means of satisfying it.

She thought of the 'death-bone', of 'death-powder'; but the effectiveness of these spells was not certain. There was only the 'werpoo', the sharp-pointed bone which kills and emerges from the wound without leaving a trace. However, unless she had the man completely in her power, Mary knew that she could not deliver the mortal blow. So she had recourse to Picky to find out if Billy liked whisky and if, as well, it was easy to get hold of a bottle.

Miss Jane's pupil carried out her mission very well; in her conversation with Billy, who liked to amuse her with various antics, she asked him if he liked whisky. The black man's eyes lit up and the answer left no doubts. It was child's play for Picky to find out where they kept the whisky; she herself found the bottles lined up on a shelf in the store, and knowing that Miss Jane was busy in the cookhouse making melon jam, she carried off a bottle under her dress.

Mary, seeing that things were working out well, began to make her 'werpoo'. For that she needed the bone of an emu or of a kangaroo. In her hunting after reptiles she often went through the paddocks lying near her hut, and she knew a place in the Boree paddock where she could find what she wanted. So she set off as if on her daily walk, with her pipe in her mouth and a tomahawk in her hand; she followed the fence for a quarter of an hour, then stopped in front of the dried body of an emu. Several weeks before, the bird had tried to clear the barrier with an ill-calculated leap and had fallen on the other side, its feet caught as if in a vice between the wires twisted into an x, and in that position had died of hunger. It was already no more than a dried mummy, and its big black claw still pointed at the sky with its three formidable toes.

Mary had soon hacked off one of the legs with her tomahawk, and back home she set to work seriously. For hours she scraped, sharpened, filed the femur, made it pointed at one end, and finished up with a sort of hollow stylus or bodkin about fifteen inches long, with a groove running almost the full length one-quarter of an inch wide with sides one-sixteenth of an inch thick. She polished it like a piece of ivory, put the final touches to it as if to a work of art, and carefully hid it away waiting for the moment to use it.

Picky was kept very busy just now; for Miss Jane had eagerly devoted herself to the religious preparation of her pupil, whom she thought would soon be ready for her first communion. Nevertheless, she promised to take into Billy's hut that very night the bottle of whisky she had so carefully hidden.

As soon as the darkness was complete, the old gin in her hiding place saw the black boy return to his hut, and shortly after heard the sound of breaking glass: Billy was opening the bottle. By and by the black man began to speak aloud, sometimes laughing like a madman or roaring like an animal. Then the words became more infrequent, more unintelligible, and Mary heard the drunken man fall onto his bed. She drew nearer, and by the light of the tallow lamp that lit the interior, she saw that the bottle was three-quarters empty.

For nearly a quarter of an hour, Billy lay moaning on his bed, ceaselessly turning over, then he gradually drifted off to sleep and finally began to snore with all his might.

Mary, in the shadows, kept watch over her prey; she made sure that the sleeping man had reached the senseless state of a log by throwing at him a few small lumps of earth that she picked up: the man didn't budge. She grew bolder, went into the hut, approached him and touched his face; the man felt nothing.

Billy slept with his face to the wall and the lamp lit up the back of his neck which emerged black and shiny from his half-open shirt collar. Mary, her eyes fixed on a spot she had just chosen, gently felt for the gap between the collarbone and the shoulder-blade at the base of the neck, placed on it the 'werpoo' which she held ready, then suddenly, pressing with all her strength, pushed it in up to three-quarters of its length. The sharp-pointed bone went straight into the heart, the man stopped snoring, that was all.

The lubra, hideous, did not remove her gaze from her victim, and once she was convinced that he had passed away, gently withdrew the 'werpoo' from the deep wound, put her thumb over the small crescent-shaped cut and held it there for a moment. When she removed it, a barely perceptible scratch appeared on the black skin: she wiped her thumb carefully, extinguished the lamp and left.

As Old Mary had foreseen, no-one suspected a thing at the station, and the bottle of whisky, decapitated and almost empty, was sufficient explanation for Billy's end; he was quietly buried at sunset.

Picky, who knew the whole story, was too much afraid of the lubra to let out her secret; she became sad and moody, and Miss Jane saw in this behaviour the contemplative state of mind in which her pupil was preparing herself for her first communion, which was to be made on the following Sunday.

Since the black boy's death, Mary had seen the rebirth of all of her tribe's superstitions, which had been somewhat suppressed for a long time; and the dead man's spirit came to visit her every night and plunge her into frightening terrors. She informed Picky of this, showing her that life was impossible for them now; the spirit had found a way of escaping from the tiny, scarcely visible wound, and was going to haunt them forever.

So one morning, Mary and Picky disappeared, never to come back.

Miss Jane was horrified when she heard the news, and her pupil's ingratitude was a great sorrow to her. But it was much worse when she noticed on going into Picky's room that she had left behind her Bible and her shoes.

(First published in *A l'autre bout du monde*, 1905)

HIS DOG

Certainly, the animal was not handsome; his wild fur, yellow and white, his crooked ears and his awkward tail formed an unprepossessing ensemble at first sight. As for his breed, an expert might have been able to find in him a mixture of collie, dingo and kangaroo dog, but he would have refused to give a firm opinion.

For Andy, the old swaggie, it was his dog, it was Treacle, that is to say everything he had in the world, everything he loved, the only creature which was attached to him; and when the animal looked at him, Andy saw in the brown circle of his eyes a deep blue reservoir of unfailing affection.

The life of one had for six years been the life of the other: since he had been a young puppy, when his paws could scarcely carry him very far, the four-legged companion had slept in a sugarbag, rocking to the steps of the swagman who was wearing out his soles and his existence on the roads of Australia. Soon the sugarbag was no longer useful and Treacle followed his master, who tried at first to shorten the distance between camps and to prolong the time in camp.

During the bad season, Andy would take whatever work he could, clearing a paddock or chopping wood; then, when the buzzing of the flies heralded the approaching heat, the tent would be transported to the banks of a river, and he would take up fishing, his favourite occupation.

Right from the beginning Treacle had taken a keen interest in this sport; as intelligent as he was ugly, he had quickly noticed that his master had his eyes fixed on the cork float. Proud of this discovery, the pup yapped with pleasure the first time he saw the cork dance and then disappear beneath the water. The fish was hooked, but a rather rough paternal hand made Treacle understand that it was sometimes necessary in this world to hide one's impressions. The dog remembered the lesson, and henceforth only his tail signalled silently that they were biting.

His education went on developing every day, moreover, most often at his expense; thus he had learnt that if the campfire was pretty to look at, the embers burnt your nose and your paws if you weren't careful. The steaming billy, he also knew, was something to be respected. In spite of everything, life for Treacle was full of varied distractions; he could catch a rabbit that didn't have too much of a start on him, and from time to time he could amuse himself chasing a kangaroo rat. The flies had early been an easy amusement, and if his attempts to snap at them with his jaws didn't always achieve the desired result, the occupation still had its charm nevertheless. But gradually he came to look at flies in a different light and realised that these beasties were a pest more than anything else.

The years passed, always the same for Andy, whose philosophy and feeble ambitions were satisfied with a life such as he had chosen, bordered by gum trees and a creek or a river.

Towards his fourth year the dog almost lost his life, and without the presence of mind of his master, the accident would have been fatal. On the bank of the Murrumbidgee where the grass was high, Treacle was prancing along gaily ahead when Andy saw him suddenly leap to one side howling with fear. A snake had bitten the dog on his left ear; Andy had the time to kill the reptile, then, holding fast to his companion, he cut off his ear where it joined the head. The animal cried out, shook his head, but quickly forgot the accident: Treacle was saved, but his looks had not been improved in the process.

Andy was growing old, his legs were beginning to drag a bit and the swag was becoming heavier for him; but the dog was still young, and although his muzzle showed more white than the rest of his person, he still kept his pup's playfulness and good humour. He would strut merrily along the road, carrying for hours a beef-bone whitened by seasons of sun and rain, and on which an ant wouldn't have found enough for a meal.

Sometimes it was a stick, a piece of bark, or even an old tin can that he would bring back to camp.

One day when they were crossing some hills where the black trunks of the ironbarks formed a sad setting full of solitude, Treacle, who was rummaging about all over the place, found a stone to his liking and took it firmly between his jaws; Andy was walking ahead, busy chasing away the flies with a leafy branch.

Two hours later when they got to a creek, Andy put the billy on the fire, and while he was waiting Treacle set down the stone at his feet. It was a piece of quartz that the dog's saliva had washed white as snow; Andy picked it up, and as he had been a miner in his youth, he looked at it carefully all over and didn't take long to notice in it a gleaming encrustation that he recognised: it was gold, all right.

That evening Andy smoked for a long time looking into the fire, and Treacle was given many pats for which he didn't seek to know the reason. When the swagman rolled himself up in his blanket, he began to dream before his eyes were closed.

Early the next day they broke camp, Andy retraced his steps and followed the path they had taken the day before. Finally, after half a day of searching, Andy thought he had rediscovered the probable spot of Treacle's find.

Some weeks afterwards, Andy had his claim marked out, and as soon as he found a partner, he began to dig his shaft.

The dog without pedigree, with no beauty, and possessing only one ear, became famous nevertheless; for Andy's mine, the 'Lucky Pup', was the talk of the district after two months.

As a result of the unexpected fortune which came their way, Andy almost went mad with joy, and several times Treacle very nearly died of indigestion.

(First published in *Sous la Croix du Sud*, 1910)

FIFTY-FIVE MINUTES LATE

A small trunk line in New South Wales: nobody knows why it was built, except the few passengers it jolts along each week. A twice-weekly service which doesn't even pay for the axle grease.

The train stopped before a platform on which there was a small shed and a water tank: the whole thing bore the name of 'Billilingora' which was proudly displayed on a long panel.

The faces which appeared at the doors seemed to be feeling the heat and looked tired and dusty. George, the conductor, was the only one to alight. He gave the mailbag to the woman who served as station master and received another one in exchange: both bags were quite limp and had nothing in their bellies.

After several minutes, a travelling salesman who was probably riding on this line for the first time asked out loud what was the reason for the hold up. No-one found enough energy to answer such a question, and anyway no-one knew. The heat had long since melted away the travelling salesman's pleasantries; he began to take it out on the people who were trying to run the New South Wales railways.

At last the train started up again with three jolts and soon reached its maximum speed: fourteen miles an hour. On either side the landscape was nothing but hillocks throwing up red bumps among the yellow grass.

The plain was dotted with clumps of thin trees, all that the miners had left behind them twenty years before. Three thousand men had dug holes in this country just as worms do in wood: they had piled up all these heaps of red earth, they had buried a whole forest which was slowly rotting away in the shafts. Now the burning sun baked the hillocks on which no grass would grow, for the clay ripped out of the ground could not get used to the light of day.

The train had been rolling along for half an hour when a man standing between the rails stopped it suddenly by making signals. George ran up beside the locomotive to see what was going on.

'Is there a doctor on board?' asked the anxious man.

'I don't think so,' said George, who knew almost all the passengers and who could guess what the rest were. 'Has there been an accident?'

'My wife took ill an hour ago.'

The passengers were all hanging out the doors; George soon verified that there was no doctor.

Mrs Kelly climbed down from a second-class compartment, with more agility than her large person would have given one to suppose, and called out to the man. She murmured several questions to him, to which he replied: 'Yes, it came over her an hour ago; the house is three-quarters of a mile from here.'

For two seconds Mrs Kelly seemed undecided, then she said to the conductor: 'George, I'm going off to look at this woman: you can wait for me if you like, or you can go on; in any case, I'm off.'

Then, turning to the passengers who were wanting to know what was happening, she asked for some whisky. This appeal was not in vain, for several bottles of different shapes, with contents of various levels, were handed to her: looking them over rapidly, she spied a bottle more than half full of liquid contents and took possession of it.

Then she followed the man in the direction of a clump of trees which could be seen dancing in the heat which rose from the ground.

'Well, I say! That's the limit!' grumbled the travelling salesman as he watched them move off.

No-one else complained: they all lived in the bush, where time is not counted in money, where a man is always ready to help his neighbour in case of need. The passengers climbed down; some farmers went off to check the sheep which were panting in their open-sided waggon; three youngsters inspected the

94

locomotive; others, strolling among the hillocks, picked up pieces of quartz to try and see if there were specks of gold in them.

During this time Mrs Kelly walked on bravely with her companion with the sun beating down overhead. The flies were terrible; it must have been 110 degrees Fahrenheit in the shade, but the woman's heavy features showed no sign of bad humour. The man explained the case to her as best he could; he said he was a miner and worked in the abandoned shafts, which gave him just enough gold to live on.

Mrs Kelly was the local Providence, everyone in the district knew her. Her sole occupation in this life seemed to be to do good, to help people who needed helping. She could be seen on the road at any hour of the day or night, going to visit a sick person, to comfort somebody with an injury or to help a poor soul pass through the black gate which closes forever. The previous month, it was she who had saved Joe Smith for his wife and five kids when he was brought back with his foot nearly cut off by the blow of an axe. Many were the sick and dying that she had assisted; many were the voices which rose in her praise.

The miner's hut was a miserable shack, mostly made of bark and old oil drums; a grubby urchin and a young dog were playing in the dust: both ran off at the arrival of the visitor.

Mrs Kelly went into the hut while the man began cutting up wood without taking his eyes off the door. After several long minutes, Mrs Kelly re-emerged.

Her face was aglow, as she called out to the miner; her kindly smile did him good. 'It's a girl, come and kiss her.'

The patient was resting and the man, seeing that everything was well, offered to go back with Mrs Kelly. He listened attentively to all her instructions; she promised to send what was necessary by the next day's train.

The miner couldn't find words to thank her; he didn't know how to show her his gratitude. Suddenly he asked: 'What is your Christian name?'

'Elizabeth,' replied Mrs Kelly.

'Well then, we'll call the child Elizabeth, and may the good Lord bless you!'

Mrs Kelly was anxiously awaited by the passengers.

'Is anything wrong?' asked one of them as soon as she was back.

'It's a big baby girl,' said Mrs Kelly, 'and all's well.'

The travelling salesman forgot his frustrations, he raised his hat and shouted: 'Three cheers for the kid!'

Thirty voices responded with three excited hurrahs while the locomotive's whistle also gave three salutes. Then the miner, choking with emotion, cried: 'Three cheers for Mrs Kelly!' Once more the empty plain resounded with hurrahs and strident whistles.

'All aboard!' cried George.

The train set off again and as the sun slipped behind the horizon, the miner watched the carriages disappear, while handkerchiefs and hats waved on to wish him good luck.

'Fifty-five minutes late,' said George to the conductor, consulting his watch. 'No matter, Australia needs more children!'

(First published in *Sous la Croix du Sud*, 1910
Translated by Patricia Brulant)

THE SPOONBILL HUT

'This morning they brought me here to the Spoonbill Hut, which is situated seventeen miles from the station and which, for some time at least, is to be my "home". Old Tom who drove me in the buggy while I led my horse by the bridle, helped me settle in.

'Backing onto the curtain of tall trees which border the creek, the hut opens its only door onto the great desert plain: from a distance, as we arrived, it made me think of a tin can left behind under the gums. It is entirely built of corrugated iron, consisting of a single room, one of whose sides is taken up by the fireplace. The earth which forms the floor is invaded by the climbing stalks of a pumpkin-vine which has grown without any help and which is beginning to climb up one of the walls.

'The first thing my eyes met is an inscription in charcoal on the door of the hut: "Look out for snakes". What a welcome!

'Tom gives me a hand to clean up the room. The swaggies have left behind newspapers, playing cards, old shoes and tin cans. Unfortunately they have made a fire with the frame which served as a bed, and there's not a single plank left of it.

'Tom, who is an old bushman, proud of showing the "new chums" what he can do, chops down a tree, and in twenty minutes, with four forked sticks, four poles and two empty sacks, he builds me a bed that is comfortable, if not elegant in shape. He is going to borrow my table from a large gum tree from which he has removed a square of bark. That is my furniture.

'I am now a boundary rider, I have to watch over the wire fencing of a 15,000 acre paddock: I must see to it that the sheep go to drink at the creek, that the fence gates are closed: when an animal dies, I must skin it and dry the hide in the shade.

'While we were having our lunch, Old Tom gives me a few

final instructions on what I have to do: once a week, on Saturdays, I go to the station to make my report to the boss and fetch some meat and provisions.

'The Hut is well named, for all along the creek the spoonbills perch in the trees or dabble in the water. They make white spots on the water darkened by the eucalyptus leaves and their cries give a bit of life to this solitude.'

'I slept well the first night, in this bed made of wood which was still alive and hadn't finished bleeding. Scamp who keeps me company now seems to me an invaluable companion. I've only had this dog for two months; but he seems to have packed into his animal heart more blind and faithful attachment than a man could show in a whole life.

'My "home" is already beginning to look less wild: I have a lamp made from a tin which once contained quince jam; it is full of tallow holding as a wick a strip torn from some old trousers. It smokes acceptably and gives a little light.

'My larder is a sack hanging from a branch by a piece of wire which passes through the cork of a bottle with a broken bottom; that stops the ants from getting to the food.

'The inscription on the door really stands out, I can't take my eyes off it; even at night I think I can read it through the corrugated iron. This morning I removed it, washed it off with a rag soaked in creek water. Even so, I feel I can still see its tipsy letters, its rising line and the S broken in two where the piece of charcoal snapped.

'All the children in this district wear thick leather gaiters: I was struck by this on the first day of my arrival. I asked the reason for it; I was told with a certain pride that this part of New South Wales had more snakes to the acre than any other; more even than Swan Hill on the Murray.

'I have always had an indefinable horror for these reptiles, even before ever seeing a live one; it is curious that Chance, which I always write with a capital, should have pushed me into this country. Despite all that I have experienced, these creatures have fascinated me since I saw them in my childhood in the illustrations to travel tales.

'Yesterday, while I was repairing a wire strand on the fence, my eyes fell on my stockwhip that I had thrown into the grass. I leapt aside so hard that my horse, tied to one of the fence-posts, snapped his bridle as he stepped back. Then I laughed at my fear while all my nerves were still taut and my heart was racing fit to burst: but really, in the grass, that twelve-foot leather thong, finely plaited in kangaroo skin, does look just like a snake.'

'Today, Saturday, I set off early for the station to fetch my provisions: it's tobacco especially that I miss. Blinker threw me yesterday when he got his two front legs caught in a rabbit-hole; my block of tobacco must have stayed on the ground, for I haven't been able to find it since.

'A pipe is a companion in the bush, its bowl is full of dreams. We watch the smoke rising, and our spirit follows our eyes, and with them, leaves the world behind, around which sad thoughts swirl heavily like thick mists. That is perhaps the secret of tobacco.

'I saw the boss at his desk. I made my report and told him that the rabbits are beginning to increase their numbers in the Gum Swamp paddock; he's going to send out the two poisoning machines next week.

'While I'm in the store, where Joe is filling up my bags of flour, tea and sugar, someone darkens the light coming in through the door. Raising my eyes, I see the graceful silhouette of a woman dressed all in white.

'She asks Joe to fill up her ink-bottle, and while the storekeeper acquits himself of his task in as pleasant a manner as possible, I stay hidden behind the sacks of flour, for I feel ashamed of my patched trousers and my coarse shirt with the sleeves rolled up to the elbows.'

'Dan and Alf, the poisoners, arrived yesterday with their machines. They have set up their tent on the creek, not far from my hut, and have mixed up the phosphorus paste which they distributed today in the paddock. I could hear for a long time the click of the mechanical knife cutting the paste into small pieces while it fell into the furrow traced by the plough that was pulled along behind each cart. The furrows go in all directions, form mazes around the warrens, cross each other and meander.

'Sitting nonchalantly on their seats, they drive their horses whistling and singing as they strew over the paddock thousands of pellets, moulded out of atrocious sufferings and death.

'Tonight, coming back to the hut, I followed these furrows; in many places the baits have gone and the rabbits, attracted by the freshly turned earth, have dug holes in it. The two men kept me company on the nights they were camped on the creek. Dan is famous at the station because of the love affair that he had with a local girl. Everyone knew Pearl O'Brien except Dan who, six months ago, was a new arrival. Pearl was almost pretty in her features, she had eyes which, judged separately, were beautiful: but the left one maintained an independent stance from the right which was the ruin of them both: Pearl was terribly cross-eyed.

'Now Dan used to go off to woo his fair lady after sundown, as soon as he had finished his meal. Each evening he would ride ten miles to get there, and as much on the way back, just so that he could say all sorts of sweet things to her on a verandah as dimly lit as it was favourable to lovers.

'But when Dan arrived one Sunday afternoon, dressed in his finest attire, his heart sank when he saw his Pearl in full daylight. For him it was the end of the idyll, for he is superstitious and a great gambler. Pearl O'Brien never saw him again.

'Joe who told me this story found it very funny: I rather felt it was sad.'

'Last night, I heard the cries of dying rabbits; the phosphorus was beginning its work slowly but surely, like a hellish drug. This morning, doing my rounds, I crossed the paddock and saw many white bellies lying still in the sun and crows everywhere, busily pecking away at the dead rabbits. The crow, in his devilish cunning, eats his fill, but without touching the intestines which would poison him.'

'Coming back for lunch, I find the boss and the young woman of the other day sitting around my fire watching the billy. I am complimented on the cleanliness of my hut. Miss X is very amused by the sardine tin which holds the soap and burst out laughing in front of my mirror which reflects like a well into which a great big stone has just been thrown.

'Her eye lights on the photograph of Penton Grange. She admires it and asks me what this fine manor house is. I tell her that it's my father's house in Devonshire. She stops laughing. She has understood that the boundary-rider of the Spoonbill Hut has a sad history and that he is hiding in the Australian bush.

"Tea oh!" calls the boss who has laid out lunch outside: without ceremony, without making me feel my position, I am invited to sit down. I am happy and yet I feel out of place: my hands with their broken nails, my fingers calloused by the wire, make me ashamed. One of my spurs is tied on with a piece of string, and it seems that in the whole paddock only that string can be seen.

'Scamp immediately made advances and had himself patted by Miss X with visible pleasure.'

'Last night the dog woke me up with a start by jumping on my bed: it was something he never does, and I immediately concluded that some danger had pushed him to seek refuge next to me. At the same time I heard a rustling on the floor of the hut: a snake. I reached out my hand towards the packing case on which the matches were, but clumsily, I spilled them under the bed. I stretched out my arm to feel for them, and in the same instant I thought of the reptile. For two hours I kept quite still, trying to see through the darkness; my roaring ears heard the rustling sound from time to time, my heart was pounding sickeningly. Scamp's muzzle sought out my hand, I stroked his head and, towards morning, I fell asleep out of sheer fatigue.

'At sunrise, I could see on the ground the snake's trail marked at certain spots: I found a hole that I had not noticed near the door and carefully blocked it up.'

'It is now almost a month since I have written a word in this diary. Sleepless nights have driven me almost mad, and several times I have felt like asking to leave this hut; but I want to have the courage of my fear. I think it must be much easier to have the other courage. I no longer sleep very much at night, though I leave my lamp alight. Scamp sleeps on my bed now, I dare not prevent him.

'Each day coming home when I pass by the swamp, it's like walking through a nightmare landscape. The grasses are tall and the trees are hollow, revealing at their base black holes into which I dare not look. The dead branches resemble snakes: there is one big tree at whose foot I see each time the shrivelled body of a large greyhound: I am afraid for Scamp and make him follow closely in my horse's shadow.'

One day this summer, about midday, a man rode up at a gallop to the station of Korubla. His face was white and his eyes full of terror. One of his wrists was wrapped in a bloody rag; the blood flowed over his hand and down his fingers.

It was the new chum from the Spoonbill Hut.

He slid rather than dismounted from the panting, sweat-covered horse and said to the boss, who had seen him first: 'I have been bitten by a snake.'

Without another word, he collapsed on the verandah of the store.

With the aid of the men the boss had him carried to a bed: they untied his bandage, but had to put it back on, for the new chum had cut his artery in his haste to make an incision. Despite all that was done, the injured man did not regain consciousness and died half an hour after his arrival. They examined the snake's

102

bite; the boss, who knew something about it, looked at the punctures, and as there were four of them, he said: 'The man died of fear: it's a carpet snake which bit him and this snake is not venomous.'

When they went to the hut to look for the new chum's belongings, they found an exercise book in which a few pages were covered with a slender, feminine handwriting.

Harry went to light his pipe with one of the pages when I took it from his hands and kept it, thinking that it might perhaps interest someone.

(First published in *Sous la Croix du Sud*, 1910)

The young Paul Wenz in 1897. He is standing in front of the fireplace in the original cottage at Nanima. Behind him is a collection of mementos from his first travels, including his time in Algeria. (*Private collection*)

Paul Wenz and his early partner William Dobson celebrating the completion of the homestead at Nanima in 1898 with a case of Krug champagne. (*Mitchell Library*)

A view of Nanima homestead when completed in 1898. Wenz and his builders made their own bricks on the site and used imported Marseilles tiles for the roof—an unusual feature for a rural homestead. (*P. Wenz, Mitchell Library*)

Paul Wenz in the store at Nanima, circa 1898. (*Mitchell Library*)

Shearers waiting to be paid at Nanima, circa 1898. (*Mitchell Library*)

Wool bales from Nanima ready to be taken to the railhead, circa 1898. *(Mitchell Library)*

Portrait of Paul Wenz by his brother Frédéric, circa 1904. (*Coll. Claude Gonin*)

Paul and Hettie Wenz in a Durban rickshaw, 1925. (*Coll. Claude Gonin*)

Hettie and Paul Wenz and writer Miles Franklin (right) at
Nanima in May 1937 (*Coll. Denis Wenz*)

Real Australians! Hettie and Paul Wenz at Nanima in the 1930s.
(*Coll. Denis Wenz*)

THE WAGGONER

At the age of five, the young girl could manage to hitch herself up onto the horse all alone, after having led it over to a tree-trunk: once in the saddle and her feet in the stirrups, she could prod the animal, who knew perfectly well in which direction the cows were to be found and, good old horse that he was, would show an angelic patience and all sorts of indulgence towards the child.

Morning and night, Jessie would go out to look for the three cows that her mother milked and, her hair blowing in the breeze, she would gallop among the tall trees in the paddock, followed by the kangaroo dog, who was always held back by his great age and numerous wounds. She helped her mother with the household chores as best she could, and like any self-respecting Australian kid, she could already set to work with an American axe on anything that an axe can chop.

The father was almost always on the road with his team of eighteen horses carrying wool, flour, provisions or fencing wire for several large stations. He was sometimes away for four months without coming back, and then one evening the mother and child would hear a still far-off sound that they quickly recognised. First it was the rumble of the wheels on the track, the pace of the horses, and finally the three whipcracks which exploded in the air like three Winchester shots.

They would run up to meet the cloud of golden dust in which the horses appeared like ghosts: they kissed the father, called each animal by its name, while the leaders, Punch and Duke, would quicken their pace as they came into the paddock they knew so well.

They would help the father to unharness; Jessie would load herself with a horse-collar that she could hardly drag along or would haul three yards of chain. The horses, freed of their harnesses, would shake themselves with pleasure and immediately head for a little heap of sand where they could romp as they pleased: there was soon a huge swell of large hooves kicking in the air and enormous rumps rolling in the pink sand.

The father would be hungry, and they would quickly sit down to table. Between mouthfuls he would tell of his journey: in the black soil plain he had got bogged down twice with seven tons of wire on board; he had passed by Sandy Ridge where five hundred miners were digging holes everywhere in order to find black opals: two men had found £400 worth in three weeks.

While the mother cleared the table and did the washing up, Jones would cut his tobacco and stuff his pipe while asking about the news of the district. The girl, sitting on her father's lap, would recount at length the story of a certain red poddy-calf, newly born, or of a tame cockatoo who had taken it upon itself to prune the two rose bushes in the little garden.

In winter, when the roads were too bad, Jones would stay a month or two on his farm clearing land and burning dead trees. He would also cart over to the front of the house a pile of firewood which would last until he next came back; he would repair the harnesses, and inspect all the bolts on his waggon; when it was necessary, he would give the vehicle a fresh coat of paint and carefully touch up the waggon's name, 'My Jessie'.

The morning would come when he would have to harness the horses, and kiss his wife and little girl: then, mounted on his black horse, he would call each animal by its name, and when all the chains were taut, he would call 'get up' and, without a jolt, the wheels would turn. His heavy two-handed whip would fire off three farewell salvos; a few minutes later he would have disappeared with his team behind the trees along the creek.

The mother and child would return to their solitary life; the nearest township was thirty miles away; the farms and stations in this district were far away from each other. Now and then drovers would pass through, driving their flocks before them; waggoners would stop their teams to have a bit of a chat; swagmen would come by asking for tea, sugar and flour.

The mother was not of a very solid constitution: one winter, on coming home, Jones found her in bed; Jessie was looking after her and had been managing the housework for a week. The sick woman soon had to be taken to the nearest hospital, forty miles from the farm. But there was nothing they could do to save her, and after a few weeks, without suffering, she crossed over the 'Great Barrier'.

Jones, left alone with the girl, did not want to stay on the farm: he sold his land, the cows, and the few items of furniture which were in the house. He got some new camping equipment, and bought a tent for Jessie, as well as a pony and a man's saddle.

The girl was eight years old when she followed her father over the endless plains; she soon got used to her new life. She had quickly learned the thousand tiny details which make life easier when you camp out in the open; without difficulty, she could light a fire of damp wood while the wind was blowing up a storm; she could bake the weekly bread on a piece of eucalypt bark. When it rained, Jones would put up the tents and dig a tiny ditch around them to drain the water: she would go to sleep listening to the raindrops drumming on the stretched canvas; in fine weather, she would sleep anywhere, and rolled up in her possum-skin rug, she would amuse herself looking at the stars and counting those which 'winked'. She loved watching the moon rise huge behind the silhouette of dead trees, and in spite of stories of bushmen blinded by its light, she loved going to sleep under its gentle glow. She also loved the big camp fire which, at night, lit up the tall branches of the gum trees, white and smooth as women's arms. The father would smoke his pipe while telling her tales of miners, grassfires, floods or long droughts.

At sunrise, while the billy was on the fire, she would help round up the horses: they would walk through tall grass wet with dew when the animals were not far from camp. When the grass was meagre, the team would often be a mile or a mile and a half away, and she would have to ride the pony to go and fetch them.

114

As a result of living with the horses, Jessie came to know them as thoroughly as her father knew them; like him, she loved them and was proud of the team. A child of the bush, she instinctively observed everything around her; she had quickly recognised the peculiarities of each animal, and she had soon seen that each one had his own well-defined personality. Punch, a sort of dappled grey mastodon, had been brought up on the bottle, and what's more, very badly brought up. From his youth he had acquired strange appetites, eating anything that a horse of good will could swallow and chewing the rest. His presence not far from the tent was always suspicious, for he had a mania for poking his nose into things.

George, the brown bay, hairy-footed like every self-respecting Clydesdale, was an incomparable worker: the only thing he insisted on was that the bit be put under his chin and not in his mouth. Duke, the heavily-built chestnut, had been completely blind for four years; he had lost his sight, Jones said, by eating wild melons on the Darling. His infirmity did not prevent him being one of the best in the team; strangely, Duke never got thin, whereas his workmates never failed each autumn to show clearly that they possessed the required number of ribs.

Jessie saw the bush animals every day; sometimes the big, soft-eyed kangaroos, sometimes the emus, simultaneously afraid and curious. She could recognise birds by their call, and was not repelled by the frill-necked lizard which looks like a nasty dream creature. She would stop beside the track to tease with a long stick some bulldog ants, whose bite is like a red-hot iron; or else she would watch a fat spider retreat into its round hole dug in the ground and shut its trapdoor. Snakes did not frighten her and she never passed one without trying to break its back with a crack of the whip.

The father, who had the soul of a bushman, had inspired the love of animals in her, except for the diabolical crows and the rabbits, which are a scourge.

For months they would travel through a corner of New South Wales where the population is scattered and the railroad has

115

not yet reached. They would encounter other waggons and sometimes travel along together, and in the evening, around the fire, they would talk long into the night, smoking tobacco and drinking tea as black as coffee. One day, a horseman warned them that a convoy of camels was approaching. For Jones, that was the signal to clear the decks for action; he seemed to be getting ready for a squall. He watched the road anxiously and in his imagination could already see his eighteen horses bolting in a crazy charge across the plain. He could see his waggon overturned and shattered to pieces; the sacks of flour split open, the chests of tea burst and the rice spread out in long patches on the red earth.

He kept his eye on the horses, and as a precaution he had made Jessie dismount from her pony. Fortunately the fears were not realised: the twenty-five camels led by the Afghan drivers passed at a respectable distance, and the horses got just enough of their scent to make them prick up their ears. The camels were each carrying two bales of wool and followed each other in file, silently, pitching and rolling. The last animal had been entrusted with a large canvas sack from which emerged the head of a small camel too young to follow the caravan.

Jessie, well positioned in her man's saddle—she didn't want any other kind—her legs stretched straight in stirrups that were too big for her, would ride forth into this world that seemed wider to her with each day. She rode over plains on which the tall grass and the trees quivered in a heat haze as if they belonged to an undersea landscape; she camped beside creeks in which the ducks, the white-plumed spoonbills and the pearl-grey brolgas lived in peace. She had passed through a town of three thousand inhabitants where she had been afraid at seeing so many people all at once, so many horses and so many houses; she had seen the Darling where steamboats sailed past towing barges piled up with wool bales which were going off to Victoria 800 miles away.

Her father had shown her the great sheds where the sheep were shorn, and the noise of the machines had frightened her;

116

hidden in a garden planted with orange trees and flowers of every colour, she had caught sight of the house of a squatter who was the owner of a million acres and of 200,000 sheep.

Jones loved the child more with every day, for she was his companion, his mate, and she brightened up the monotony of the road and the great silence of the bush. She had become a clever little housewife, taking care of the cooking and even knowing how to make cakes, which she baked in the camp oven. She helped him round up the horses and harness them, and she soaped up the washing on Sunday mornings while they were resting in camp.

One day Jones left Jessie in charge of the camp and set off at daybreak on his horse: at sunset he came back after having done sixty miles. A compelling reason had pressed him to make this foray: he had no more tobacco, and for the first time in his adult life he had had to go without smoking his pipe.

The waggoner had taken charge of her education; he had taught her to read with the advertisements of three-week-old newspapers. His baggage of knowledge was not heavy, and often the child's questions greatly embarrassed him. He particularly gave her object lessons, showing her the Southern Cross and its two pointers; he told her what he knew of the habits of bush animals, and explained to her how you found gold. On this subject he really knew what he was talking about, for the gold he had found in his youth had brought him in about £30 sterling an ounce!

The winter rains made travelling difficult; often in summer the grass was sparse and he had to carry cut hay to feed the team. But Jones, like the Australian that he was, had learned to be philosophical, to take difficulties calmly, or rather to consider them as routine things forming part and parcel of life's scheme.

In the morning, when the grass was silver with dew, when the barely risen sun seemed like a splash of gold through the trees along the creek, they would emerge numb with cold from inside the tent, stir up the fire and quickly drink a billy of scalding tea. In the mist which smelled so nicely of cool weather, the horses were merely distant shadows and Paddy's bell, which tinkled every second, indicated that chewing was going on without any waste of time.

For the waggoner and his daughter, this bell was what the village church bell is for others. Its ringing followed them everywhere, it carried in its thin brass shell a note of gaiety and peace which only rang in times of rest, between the setting of the sun and its rising.

Often at night Jones and the child would wake up and listen ... then like a feeble echo they would hear the bell. From the chill of dawn their first thought would be for the bell; was it far away?

Moondooroo had 110,000 sheep to shear that year. In the immense corrugated iron shed, the forty-eight machines, guided by as many shearers, were roaring like powerful beasts, and their gleaming steel seemed to caress the sheep's bodies as they snipped off their wool with jaws moving at 380 revolutions per minute. The animals struggled and bleated their protests, and became whiter each time the machine passed over their skin. They were handled and turned over like large fruits being peeled, while their snowy fleeces spread out like frothy suds on the floor shiny with lanolin and machine oil.

Here and there a long red gash, a wound, would appear on a sheep's skin: the shearer would call out 'Tar!', and a lad would run up and daub the wound. Other boys endlessly came and went, carrying off the fleece to the sorting tables and sweeping the floor.

At the other end of the shed, two steam-powered presses were kept filled up with fleeces which they compressed into bales whose jute wrapping was stretched to bursting.

Outside, in the yards, there was the calling of the men and the barking of dogs in the middle of a thick, brown, peppery dust kicked up by the panicky sheep. Here, they were marking the shorn sheep with an 'M'; there, they were preparing to bring into the shed fresh sheep for the next day's shearing.

118

In the shed, from six in the morning to six at night (except at smoko and meal times), there was the din of bleating and shouts overlaid with the roar of the machines in a stifling atmosphere thick with the panting of sixty men and 2,000 sheep.

Shearer number seven was the 'ringer', shearing his 120 sheep in a day; he was not only the man who shore the most sheep, but also the one who shore them best. Number thirty-three could shear almost as many as the ringer, but in the position allotted to him the pine floor seemed more like mahogany, it was so red with blood.

The ringer was somehow part of his machine; he made regular scything movements, his shears cut long swathes, leaving the skin pink, skirting delicately round the thighs so as not to cut the hamstrings, working gently around the ears and taking off the facial wool without touching the eyelids.

You hear tell of shearers who have done 200 sheep in a day; but there are Queensland sheep with no wool on the legs or the belly; the Moondooroo beasts had yankee blood in their veins and fleeces thick with folds which the shearers generally hated and which they nicknamed 'accordion'.

At six o'clock the steam whistle announced that the long day's work was done; the machines stopped one after another, and the shearers and rouseabouts left the shed with a bent back and a weary spirit.

In the violet of nightfall, the camp fires were glowing like forges, their blue smoke drifting lightly up to the first stars. A great calm was falling, magnifying the voices and laughter of the men sitting down to eat in the hut.

Two hundred yards away, on the river bank, stood the waggoners' camp. These men, about fifteen in number, were awaiting their turn to load the Moondooroo wool in order to transport it to the railway, 175 miles away. Their camp was like that of some wild tribe: twenty big waggons with scarlet-painted wheels were lined up beneath the trees, while tents, bark huts and shelters made of branches were scattered here and there. A whole crowd of women and children moved about among the

119

huge camp fires heaped with white ashes in which whole tree-trunks were burning. Dogs, goats and their kids, and chickens completed the population of this ephemeral village. Several among the waggoners owned two waggons: the paddock which lay not far from the camp was, at that very moment, being close trimmed by the three hundred horses that made up their teams.

All the waggons bore a name, like boats: there was 'Good Boy' and 'Flying Dutchman' which belonged to Greenhalgh. 'Try Again' was owned by Bill Ford, the first waggoner who, fifteen years before, had taken on the 150 miles which separated Wambarala from Pancaira. He had got through with his waggon to Pancaira; but the speartip he was carrying in his shoulder had made him swear like a Turk, even though he had repaid with a lead bullet the black who had thrown this hardwood sliver at him.

Mick Nolan was the owner of 'Get There'; Long Jack had 'Star of the West'. But Jones had the finest of all the waggons, 'My Jessie'.

He had ordered it from Bennett, the best cartwright in New South Wales, and he had christened it with the kid's name. The back wheels were six foot six in diameter, the hubs and spokes were of ironbark and the wheel-rims of blue gum; the bodywork and the double shafts were of spotted gum. At rest or under way, 'My Jessie' always looked new and clean; all the bolts were screwed up tight, everything was greased; nothing rattled, nothing creaked. The waggon could carry fifteen tons: Jones had paid £120 sterling for her, and everywhere he went they recognised 'My Jessie' and her model team; besides, the six-inch-wide ruts were enough to announce Jones's presence in the district.

Not without some envy, Jones was admired in the waggoners' camp, for his waggon and his team were equally unrivalled. He was also envied for his daughter Jessie, who was treated somewhat as the queen of the camp. Nolan's wife might well keep goats, Greenhalgh's wife might well have a Wertheim sewing machine decorated with golden arabesques and blue flowers; but the little Jones girl had the best kept tent and the most complete set of

120

cooking utensils. Ford's wife even went so far as to claim that Jessie ate and drank only out of porcelain; but the old busybody was well known for her gossipy tongue and for the imagination with which she was afflicted.

The life of the camp was the life of a small town, except that they only got news once a week: this scarcity of communications with the outside world in no way prevented gossip or rumours.

Without exactly having their 'at-home' days, these ladies gave teas to which each brought her own pannikin. These little gatherings furnished the occasion to air the dresses kept in tin trunks dented by years of knocking around. There was no lack of entertainment; the shearers gave concerts and even balls in the shed. Nobody noticed the odour of greasy wool or the bleating of penned-up sheep; the accordion made them all waltz on the greasy floor, and not even pipe smoking was forbidden.

Sometimes a pedlar's caravan would turn up: within twenty minutes his stock of cigarettes would be sold out. The shop on wheels would be besieged by the men as well as the women; they hadn't been able to buy pipes for two months; they hadn't fingered a yard of flannel or calico for such a long time.

One evening, a 'variety company' composed of a blind man and a youth gave an open-air performance. The program comprised gramophone pieces in which Melba and Caruso alternated with songs that were more American than comical. A magic lantern paraded Queen Victoria, the murderer Deeming, and Chamberlain. Everybody attended the performance, and since cash was scarce, they signed their name on a list, next to sixpence or a shilling, and the variety company received three or four pounds from the manager, who advanced the total subscription.

The machines continued to whirr and grind and nip off the white fleeces which were progressively pressed into bales; then the bales, numbered and bearing the mark of the station— Moondooroo in a diamond—, were loaded onto the waggons, and formed a three-storey pyramid firmly held down by ropes tightened by means of wooden levers and tourniquets.

One after another, the waggons set off jerkily, looking for all the world like schooners loaded to the gunwales. When Jones's waggon was loaded up and ready to leave, the shearers stopped their machines and stood up straight, still holding between their legs their half-shorn sheep; the rouseabouts had left their tables to watch 'My Jessie' set out with sixty bales on board.

The team was handsome, the animals all in their places, with their collars already on, but their chains were still loose. Jones knew they were all watching his team, he felt proud. Jessie, sitting astride her horse, was examining the harnesses as if she was making a formal inspection: she looked at her father. Jones made a sign, and with the girl calling the lead horses and then the others by name, the chains set taut, their hocks bent and their necks strained forward. All these efforts united into one seemed, as at the start of a race, to be waiting for a signal. The child gave it, and the 'Get up!' commanded in a firm voice set the whole mass into motion: the big wheels left the bed they had dug in the red earth and the waggon took off, hailed by the wild cheers of the shearers and rouseabouts.

The boss of Moondooroo had asked Jones to get the load to the railroad by the end of the month, whatever the cost; for the wool prices were tending to fall and he wanted to sell as soon as possible. The distance from the station to the rail-head was about 175 miles, which Jones meant to cover in eighteen days if the weather permitted and if nothing broke on the way.

The road was fairly flat, cut now and then by low sandhills and small rises topped with pine woods. The clumps of scattered trees made spots of shade and neutral green under the blinding sun; there were grey mulgas that the cattle had trimmed into parasols, 'leopard trees' with spotted bark, 'beefwood trees' whose freshly cut wood is the colour of meat, wild fuchsias, and saltbush with pale blue-green leaves.

During the first week the waggon followed the river; they had not yet left the limits of Moondooroo. They passed one of the artesian bores, the boundary-rider's hut, then the two wooden crosses planted under a quandong at the spot where two swagmen had died of thirst in 1888.

Jones and Jessie followed behind the waggon, sometimes on horseback and sometimes on foot; the road was good, there was no lack of grass; they were covering about ten miles a day.

On the sixteenth day the sun rose in a leaden sky and stayed imprisoned in a red haze. The horses sweated and panted. Jones and Jessie felt a great heaviness weighing on their shoulders.

Towards three o'clock in the afternoon, a dark wall rose up in the west and seemed to be drawing nearer: the sky disappeared under the thick veil which turned purple as it gradually spread out more and more.

A sandstorm, a 'Darling downpour', was about to burst on them; you could already smell an odour of damp dust, you could see half a mile away the trees twisting in the wind whose roar could already be heard.

Jones turned his horses around so as to shelter them as much as possible, halted them, and tied down tightly anything that could have given a hold to the windstorm.

They were on a low hill topped with dead trees when the blast of red sand hit them with all its force: it was so dark that you would have thought it was nightfall.

Jones had told Jessie to lie down on the ground, had completely rolled her up in a blanket, and had told her not to move. Crouching a little way off, he himself kept his eye on the horses, even though he realised that it would have been impossible for him to stop them if fear had seized them.

For a quarter of an hour the red tempest blew in all its fury, then ceased as if by sorcery while fat drops fell onto the windswept ground.

Jessie emerged from her blanket, and seeing that calm had returned, she went over to the team. A dead tree blown down by the storm had fallen right next to the waggon: the child suddenly noticed her father trapped under one of the broken stumps. The man had been killed outright: his life had been snatched away, with no visible injury, no trace of suffering on his face.

123

Jessie tried to free the body, but she saw that that would be impossible without the aid of an axe. She went to look for the tool and, choking back her sobs, attacked the stump: the dead wood was hard to cut into, and it was only after twenty minutes of work that she managed to get the body out.

When Jessie saw that it was all quite over, she wept, holding tight to the dead man's inert hand. A little while later she thought of the horses, unhitched them and took off their harnesses, then seeing them head for the creek which was not far off, she set up between the waggon's twin shafts the tarpaulin which served as a feeding-trough and filled it up with chopped hay.

It was a cruel and lonely vigil for this twelve-year-old girl; but the moment came when charitable sleep plunged her into oblivion.

As soon as dawn broke, she experienced the awakening of a child who takes a long time to pass from sleep into wakefulness: then reality loomed up before her.

She relit the fire, prepared a feed for the team, and mounted on her horse, set off to search for them along the creek.

Punch, the dappled grey, hauled his master up onto the top of the pyramid of bales, and Jessie covered the body with her blanket and secured it tightly. The storm had brought down the temperature; it was almost cold.

For a day and a half, the team led by the child kept up a good pace, for the load had to be delivered to the railhead before noon the next day; Jones's horse followed behind the waggon, its saddle empty, the reins tied to the left stirrup.

That Saturday morning, although the main street of Gandoola was full of movement and traffic, the horsemen and buggies pulled over to let the waggon and its team pass through.

The towering pile of bales teetered at the slightest jolt; the waggon and its wheels bore the dust of a long journey just as the ship arriving in port is covered with a rust that is its glory. In spite of their dusty harnesses, the horses cut a fine figure, and the girl leading them with her voice rode by gloomily, her face hidden under the brim of her broad hat.

124

And sitting bravely in her saddle, Jessie saw, as through a mist, ahead up there, at the end of an endless street, the station, the goal, the end of a long journey.

The team passed through the gate, drew up alongside the goods shed and halted on the child's command.

Jessie handed the receipt to the employee, then as her eye fell on the black horse whose saddle was empty, she slipped gently from her mount and fainted.

(First published in *Sous la Croix du Sud*, 1910)

UNPUBLISHED TEXTS

THE GAZELLE

For the third time Harry Stanford looked at the impeccably arranged tea-table that a well-schooled servant had laid out before retiring. His eyes left the sparkling silver and immaculate linen to rest with pride upon the walls decorated with hunting trophies. The Piccadilly taxidermist had delivered them the day before, and Harry had spent his morning hanging them. The rhinoceros head, the piece of which he was most proud, was well positioned; the light from the large window shone straight into the treacherous and cunning little eyes while the nasal horn rose up enormous and menacing. The wild buffalo with the massive skull, the black Rhodesian antelope, and a koodoo with long twisted horns completed this collection. A fine gazelle head in which the glass eyes had kept a liquid, living look seemed to have the place of honour above the dining table.

Stanford was a handsome type of Englishman: his big grey eyes shot occasional flashes which suggested something cruel; his smile, with his too perfect teeth, gave the same impression.

He had been back from Africa barely a month: he had spent almost a year on safari in pursuit of everything that could be struck down by a bullet.

Once again, Harry stopped before the tea-table, glanced at his watch, adjusted a spoon and removed a biscuit which seemed to him to disturb the harmony of the platter which had been artistically arranged by his butler. His mouth was still full when the telephone rang. The effort of swallowing prevented him from cursing this intrusion aloud: he managed however to speak distinctly in answering the call.

'Yes, Eva, you're running late . . . yes . . . I see, all right then, in three-quarters of an hour. See you then.'

He lit a cigarette, sank back into the deep armchair and was

129

just about to start reading *The Field* when there was a ring at the door of his flat. He went to open it and was almost knocked over by the welcoming embrace of a visitor who was obviously happy to see him again.

'Thea!'

'Yes, it's me,' said the young lady. 'I had to come upon your photograph in the papers and read the account of your adventures in order to learn that you were back in London. Not a word to tell me of your arrival! One single letter in a whole year! Oh Harry! How could you forget your old chum like that?'

He made her sit down, but had no opportunity to excuse himself, for the reproaches continued to rain down, and Thea's voice was trembling slightly.

'It's true,' he managed to say at last, 'I am a brute, darling, but if you knew what it's like on safari, always stuck in camp, tired, worn out by the blacks, the mosquitoes and the hundreds of other insects.'

'At least,' said the young woman casting an eye around the walls, 'you had as much sport as you liked. If it's sport to kill lots of poor beasts in order to hang them on the wall and show them off to friends who've never shot so much as a partridge.'

'It's very exciting,' said Harry, 'but you love animals too much to understand. You need endurance and courage all the same . . .'

'The poor wild beasts have all that, only they don't have any rifles . . .'

'But they defend themselves, they attack.'

'For one hunter killed by a buffalo,' retorted Thea, 'there are more than 500 beasts slaughtered and photographed with gentlemen in helmets and shorts and a rifle over their arm. Oh yes! we Britishers love animals!'

The young woman suddenly noticed the gazelle's head. 'Harry! You're not going to tell me you killed that dear little thing!'

Harry confessed with a nod. 'She gave me more trouble than the rhinoceros . . . She was still breathing when I caught up to her . . . and I believe she wept real tears when I found her wounded.

Fortunately my shot didn't ruin the head.'

He looked at the clock and discreetly consulted his wristwatch. 'And you, Thea, tell me about yourself. What have you been doing all this time?'

'I have often thought of you, I have been going to lectures, to cooking classes, and I have done a lot of work at home. Harry, do you remember, when we were tots, our experiments with confectionery? We used to melt some caramel in the lid of a biscuit tin . . . we used to burn our tongues, and it was bitter!'

Harry smiled, and added some little comment, but his mind was elsewhere.

'You must be expecting someone,' said Thea, 'I would have loved to chat with you a while longer: but that will be for another day. Besides, I have heaps of errands to do today. You'll let me know when I can come back again.'

Harry had stood up; he took three steps on the carpet, of which he seemed to be studying the pattern. All at once he said: 'Thea darling, I have something to tell you: I met a charming woman on the boat coming back; we seem to have the same tastes and our opinions tally. We are engaged.'

Thea stood up stiffly, then sat down again. In an expressionless voice she said: 'Harry, I wish you both every happiness.'

The man lit up a cigarette; he could thus keep some sort of composure, and each puff of smoke was a barrage behind which he could take cover for a few seconds.

Thea had got a grip on herself: 'So, Harry, our little episode is finished? This ring that you gave me and that I have been wearing for years . . .'

'Darling, we were children then, with no idea of what life really was. We were just great chums, it wasn't a real engagement . . . and anyway, I'm ten years older than you.'

While he was speaking to her very gently, as if to a young girl, Thea slowly caressed her ring. When the time came to leave she asked for a glass of water, and while he went to fetch it, she slipped the ring over one of the slender horns of the gazelle.

She kissed Harry, her eyes shiny but holding back their tears,

131

and the man felt the young woman's fingers tighten on his arms. He only just heard the 'Adieu, dear' that she whispered.

'Goodbye,' Harry corrected her. And the door closed behind her. The minutes passed. He felt relieved: he had dreaded this encounter, that is why he had delayed so long in writing to Thea. She hadn't taken it all too badly, he thought, she'd forget. Poor kid!

Suddenly the doorbell rang out violently and at the same time there was a loud knocking at the door.

Eva, his fiancée, fell into his arms, pale, shocked, with a wild look in her eyes. 'Oh God, it's horrible!' Then she sobbed and collapsed into the armchair.

'Harry! it's frightful . . . fifty yards from your door . . . this big omnibus coming towards me, then a woman run over on the roadway . . . and a bit further on, her little red hat . . .'

'With a black feather?' asked Harry, his eyes suddenly distraught . . .

'Yes, with a black feather.'

The man was about to race towards the door, but the woman stopped him roughly. The two of them stood there motionless when suddenly they heard an approaching siren: the ambulance drove past below the windows, insisting on its right of way; then the siren slowly died away.

The woman seemed to regain her composure: she was still trembling, but in her large dark eyes something seemed to have replaced the panic. She wanted to know. 'What made you ask whether she had a black feather in her hat?'

Her voice had become harsh, her face nasty.

'Thea left here a few minutes before . . . a childhood friend . . .'

'What did you do to her? I saw her throw herself deliberately and without hesitation under the omnibus. Was it . . . Oh, do say something!'

Harry wasn't listening, he was on the telephone asking for the hospital at the end of the street, the closest to the site of the accident. 'Yes, a young woman . . . black suit, red hat. Yes . . . dead on arrival?'

132

'I'm racing off to the hospital,' he said to Eva as he took his hat. 'I'll be back soon.'

Once he had left, the woman looked around her, then going over to the table where she intended to write a few words, her eyes fell on the gazelle head. On the left horn gleamed a gold ring engraved with an ivy wreath. On the inside she could read: 'Harry to Thea, June 1929.'

She replaced the ring, then taking off her own ring, a circle of platinum holding a sapphire between four claws, she slipped it over the other horn.

She got up, powdered herself in front of a small mirror, redid her lipstick. As she walked past the tea-table she looked at the two cups of fine porcelain, picked up one and smashed it on the floor.

Eva opened the door, closed it gently behind her, and once she was in the street, she hailed a taxi.

Nanima,
5 March 1936

LONE JOE

Lone Joe looked at the board which served as his calendar and stuck a used match in the twenty-first hole. He had rarely got the date wrong, except once when he had missed out the whole month of August; an error which, in any case, had in no way upset the routine of his existence.

Lone Joe had never heard of Diogenes: he would have been interested in the philosopher, for the two of them had closely related ideas on the simple life and on humanity. By dint of having seen his fellow creature under every latitude, in white, yellow, or black, Joe had finally arrived at the conclusion that the whole series was a failure. He must have had good reasons not to like his earthly brothers, for he was himself a man of mild character, naturally honest without the least effort; he had never done any harm to anyone, had committed no crime, had never loved a woman.

The few people who saw him from time to time at Talarinda wondered how a person possessing all his faculties could go and bury himself ten miles away from the township, on the edge of an empty plain in an isolated gully where thirty years before miners had searched for gold, then had disappeared leaving behind gaping holes and hillocks of yellow, barren earth.

Joe still found a little gold, but rarely spoke of it, for he didn't want neighbours at any price.

He understood the primitive life to have more comfort than Diogenes; his bark hut had more room than a barrel, and four forked sticks, two poles and two sacks formed his bed. Crates of many provenances completed the furniture, and the pots and pans had once held oil from Sumatra.

In one of the mine shafts there was water that was drinkable and always fresh: in this empty spot, that was worth its weight in gold.

Joe had a companion, an old horse who knew the creaking sound of the crank handle and who would cease grazing while the drinking trough filled up.

Every morning the miner undertook a risky descent of twenty feet down a ladder which he had made up out of wire twisted into a cable and rungs made from pieces of old crates. The ladder was solidly fixed to a tree which had grown beside the hole; but it didn't look any the less like a piece of gymnasium equipment that few people would have tried out without hesitation.

The solitude in which he lived allowed Joe to reread often the book of his existence. The first pages were still scarcely opened, their contents were vague. He could look back on the dreary childhood of an orphan, with no great joys and out of which he had suddenly emerged one day, as from a dark wood. All at once he had been dazzled by the bright sun and his lungs had filled with the salty air, while the offshore wind whipped his body and made his heart beat faster.

Newcastle, Madeira, Manaos or the Cape had merely been stopovers for him during which the noise of the propeller had given way to the whining of cranes unloading coal or cargo. Docks were alike the world over, the ugliness of the bond stores and warehouses was the same everywhere; only the smell of coconut oil in Ceylon was different from that of rotten fish in Shanghai or that of over-ripe watermelons in Naples. A few hours ashore revealed that the bars of Nagasaki exhibited the same bottles as those of Dakar.

The years had telescoped in his memory, they were so much alike: after twenty years of sailing the sea had worn him out.

He had disembarked in Adelaide just as he would have landed in Buenos Aires; he sought out a quiet corner where his back pay would allow him to live independently. After wandering for two years he had chosen this gully in South Australia which had long since been abandoned by men.

Once at the bottom of his shaft, by the light of a candle, Joe would work away with his pick and shovel and fill up the two ox-hide buckets which he would haul up as necessary by means of a steel rope. Now and then the light from his candle would shine back from a tiny nugget which the man carefully stowed in a tin box still bearing the trademark of a brand of cigarettes.

Every Saturday (the Sundays were marked in advance by a new match) he would hitch up his horse to a vehicle which illustrated, as did the harness, that blind faith which Australians place in Providence. At the end of ten miles of a track that only his wheels had travelled over for the past three years Joe, or rather his horse, would stop before the corrugated iron cube that was the Talarinda store.

A rather poorly patronised hotel and two dwellings made up the village at that time: three skinny peppercorn trees dropped their translucid shade onto the red sand. This agglomeration of a few inhabitants was all that remained of an ephemeral rush to an Eldorado. In the midst of some ruined shacks could be made out a square construction which had resisted time: its only door, still proud of its solid hinges, indicated a prison; it was proof that Talarinda had once attained a certain degree of civilisation and prosperity.

When Joe came into the store, the shopkeeper was just weighing on the counter scales little Elsie, aged eight months, who had been brought in by her elder sister. Twenty-three pounds of Elsie and ten pounds of potatoes were loaded into the pram, and the wheels, now bare of their rubber rim, creaked under the burden.

The miner ordered his supplies, put the lot into a sack and paid the shopkeeper without encouraging him in a discussion of the latest news, which held no interest for him.

His hut, his mine shaft and his horse formed the framework of his existence. He loved animals, he knew all the birds in the gully, and the drinking trough, never dry, attracted them every day at their own time. The dollar bird regularly arrived in the middle of October and streaked the blue sky with its flight as jagged as Jupiter's thunderbolts.

The pelican in his majestic gliding would announce that rain was going to fill the lake eighty miles to the north; the curlews would weep at night when the weather was about to change. The frill-necked lizards, antediluvian little monsters as horrible as they were harmless, would appear as soon as spring came, still thin from their long fast and slow-moving from their hibernation: attracted by the sun, the goannas would also come out of the hollow trees.

Joe also knew the insects: the ants that sorted the seeds, which they would leave to germinate before carrying them off to their cellars as food for the young. He could spy out the tight-fitting trapdoor which the spider pulled to after her like the hatch on the conning tower of a submarine. He always kept his hut thoroughly swept, for he feared the little red-back spider even more than the brown snake that he had found one morning at the bottom of his mine.

Joe's culinary methods were those of many bush people, and the utensil which opened the tins of food was for him an object of the first necessity. His very sweet tea was the colour of coffee before turning muddy with the addition of some milk which dribbled thickly out of a small tin can.

One day as the miner was finishing his meal, he stopped with his fork in mid-air and his mouth gaping at the sight of a young goanna which, from two yards away, was watching him with its shining eyes, neck tense, head erect, its long thin tongue popping in and out without a pause.

With a barely perceptible movement Joe dropped a few scraps of bully beef which the goanna gobbled up in the twinkling of an eye. A whole spoonful went that way, and as the big lizard still seemed to be waiting, the man gave it what was left at the bottom of the tin, after which the animal sauntered sinuously away.

The visitor came back the next day and those which followed: at the end of a week Joe understood that he had been adopted.

She was baptised Clementine, a name dear to miners. Clementine turned up promptly at mealtimes. Within a few months she grew and fattened visibly; she became less timid and allowed

Joe to stroke his finger over her scaly skin striped with wide bands of yellow and black. Every day she would find her place laid: one tin full of water and another containing some meat.

Joe sometimes came to forget about his toil, and without his realising it at first, Clementine brought a real change into his life.

It was remarked on at Talarinda that he was buying more tinned food and that he was drinking his glass of beer at the Royal as if he was in a hurry, as if somebody was waiting for his return.

Clementine was in fact waiting for him, and the dust in the front of the door of his hut was marked with criss-crossing tracks and the scorings of sharp claws which looked as though they might have belonged to fifteen goannas.

She thrived and took on the proportions of a young crocodile: she was more than three feet long, and her beautifully patterned skin made her a most presentable specimen of the monitor lizard. It was most likely that Clementine looked elsewhere for distractions and extra food, for she had come back numerous times bearing lacerations and pecking wounds, no doubt received in the attempted theft of cockatoos' eggs.

That afternoon, while Joe was watering his horse before going back down into his mine, he saw the horse raise his head and prick up his ears. Then Joe noticed a man approaching heavily laden with a swag and wearily swinging a billy at the end of his arm.

The man was younger than his wrinkles. The way he had rolled up his tent and blanket and his heavy English farmer's boots immediately gave him away as a new chum.

Joe knew what the stranger wanted: he took him into his hut, put the billy on the fire, and offered him something to eat. Then he left him, showed him where the tobacco was and told him that he would be back before nightfall.

The sun was low when Joe climbed back up the ladder. He threw a bucket of water over himself and took the small track that led to his dwelling.

The light of the setting sun suddenly revealed to him a long white patch on the trunk of the eucalyptus which was near the hut. He rubbed his eyes and distinctly saw what appeared to be a strip of bark torn off the tree.

He realised what it was at once, for as he drew near he could see the rusty nails on which was stretched, still fresh, the goanna's skin.

There was a sort of roar in the gully: the man came out of the hut and saw Joe rushing at him with wild eyes and clenched fists. Without being able to utter a word, the miner pointed to the tree trunk.

The man said: 'He came at me, I broke his back with a stick.'

Joe, beside himself, rushed into the hut and came out straight away with his Winchester in his hand. 'Get the hell out of here before I shoot,' yelled the miner.

The new chum shouldered his pack and went off straight ahead as fast as he could, without knowing where he was going.

Night had fallen, and Lone Joe was still sitting on his bed, his knotty hands clasping each other so tight that their veins were swelling up. As if dazed by a heavy blow, he was trying to unravel the reality of what still seemed to him a nightmare. Suddenly he got up, lit his lantern and made a circuit of the hut. He found Clementine's body, already being attacked by ants: he dug a small grave then extinguished the light. He begged the darkness to conceal from him something of all this horror as he covered the flayed animal with her skin and filled the hole.

For two whole days Joe didn't eat: he drank tea. He understood all that this creature had meant to him for two years, her daily presence had become a part of his existence. For the first time in his life, he the orphan, without friends, without ties of any sort, felt in the loss of one of the Good Lord's creatures a sorrow which suddenly made him hanker after the void. His body as well as his soul seemed to him to be empty of everything that awakened feeling in them. He continued to drink tea because he was thirsty; hunger, which is above all the urge to live, made itself felt; but he ignored it.

As for the one who had committed this abominable thing and who, in Joe's eyes, was nothing less than a murderer, he didn't dare think of him, and chased him from his thoughts each time the vision reappeared. When he had seen him flee from his Winchester in the direction of the wide and waterless desert plain, his anger was too fresh and too strong to prevent the man from going off to die in the shade of a saltbush.

On the third day, Joe was just about to go down into his shaft when he saw the vagabond coming towards him. He had gotten rid of his swag and carried only his billy. He raised his free arm, his hand open in a sign of submission. His eyes crazed, his lips cracked with dust, he went straight to the trough, filled his billy and raised it to his lips. Joe had to struggle with him to prevent him from drinking, for he well knew the danger: he dragged him into his hut and gave him some tea in small doses, by the spoonful. Soon the man collapsed onto the bed and fell into a heavy sleep.

Seated on a chair Lone Joe watched the sleeper for a long time, amazed at seeing him again under his roof. Sleep had not erased the suffering that shaped the vagabond's face, and an immense pity seized Lone Joe at the sight of this wreck of a man.

A ray of light fell on the calendar at the bedhead: the miner realised that for three days he had forgotten to mark the date; he moved the match and discovered that tomorrow would be the 25th—Christmas Day!

Lone Joe looked down again at the sleeping man as still and emaciated as a corpse. Gently, carefully, he arranged the filthy pillow.

November 1934

JACK LONDON

In 1909 at the end of their long cruise on the *Snark* we had the pleasure of meeting Jack London and his wife in Sydney. We had read several of his books, and we easily recognised him as the man who had written *The Call of the Wild* and *The Sea Wolf.*

The few days that we were able to spend with them are ones we shall never forget. Of medium height, but built like a Hercules, Jack London possessed in his eyes and in his whole person a strange fascination which drew you to him and didn't let go.

He was the apostle of energy, of dynamism, of struggle! He left us one evening to go off with his wife to see a boxing match at the Stadium. They returned from there enchanted, the both of them, with the fine punches that had been exchanged.

His youth had prepared him well for the battle of life; he had eaten enough raging bull to have a good stomach and powerful jaws, which are indispensable for finding one's way through the thick jungle of existence.

He worked at his table all morning, having given himself the task of writing every day a certain number of lines. Mrs Jack typed them on the machine as he went.

At one o'clock we were received into his room, where there awaited us some cocktails expertly mixed by his Japanese boy.

His adventures on the Klondyke, his experiences as a reporter during the Russo–Japanese war as well as his turbulent youth had made him independent of many of the conventions of society. The starched collar and the stiff-fronted shirt had never been part of his wardrobe, and when he put on his smoking-jacket in the evening, it was with a silk shirt and soft collar of the same fabric.

The meals that we took with him were not copious, for we

were there to listen to him, and the waiter himself appeared to be distracted as he passed the salad.

Jack London had a weakness for good coffee, and as such a thing is generally unknown in Australia (it is only appreciated when mixed with about 60% of chicory), we were hoping to have him and his wife taste the coffee that we roast ourselves on the station.

Unfortunately the plans were changed and we could not receive the Londons under our own roof.

On the eve of our departure for Europe we had seen the *Snark* anchored in Rose Bay, having just arrived from the Solomon Islands. The next day, when the *Van Spilbergen* which was taking us to Java passed within a few cables' length of the *Snark*, the brave little boat signalled us 'bon voyage', a touching gesture of friendship that Jack London and his wife addressed to the 'Wenzies', as they called us.

I admired the man and his work with all sincerity; I wanted my fellow countrymen to be able to share my admiration. That's why I translated *Love of Life*.

Somewhere in the Pacific a man was sailing his small schooner solo and suddenly found himself in difficulties that he could not overcome alone. After some hours he finally saw a barque approaching: he hailed it and soon after there climbed onto his deck a man with a thick head of hair. They spent some time together, and just as he was about to return to his barque the stranger noticed a book lying on a seat in the cabin. It was *The Valley of the Moon.*

'Do you like it?' he asked.

'Yes,' replied the schooner's owner, 'I only have books by him on board.'

'By *me*,' corrected the other man, and Jack London introduced himself.

SELECTED LETTERS

CORRESPONDENCE
WITH ANDRE GIDE

INTRODUCTORY NOTE

André Gide was born in Paris on 22 November 1869, the only son of wealthy Protestant parents. His father died when Gide was eleven. He was mostly educated by private tutor, but completed his secondary education in 1887 at the Ecole Alsacienne, where he met Paul Wenz.

A precocious, delicate, introverted youth, Gide began to compose poetry at the age of twenty and soon gravitated to the Symbolist group around Mallarmé. In 1892 he was exempted from military service on account of his health, and the following year he made the first of many visits to North Africa, where he discovered the homosexual dimension of his personality. In 1895 he married his cousin Madeleine Rondeaux and began to establish a reputation as a novelist and critic. A man of independent means, Gide devoted his life to literature and travel and consolidated his reputation as a writer with his 1902 novel *L'Immoraliste*. In 1908, Gide and a group of friends founded the *Nouvelle Revue Française*, which soon became known as the leading intellectual and literary journal in France, and later went on to help found the prestigious publishing house of Gallimard.

Paul Wenz re-established contact with Gide during his stay in France in 1909, and although they don't seem to have been particularly close during their school days, Gide became interested in Wenz's life in Australia and also took an interest in his writing. Thus began a correspondence which lasted well into the 1930s, by which time Gide had emerged as a well-known international figure; although much of this correspondence is now lost, the surviving letters indicate that it was indeed a literary correspondence.

Wenz introduced Gide to the work of Henry Lawson and Jack London among others, and Gide published Wenz's story 'Le Charretier' in the NRF in 1910 and oversaw the publication by Gallimard of his translation of London's Love of Life in 1914.

Gide also arranged introductions for Wenz to a number of British writers.

After 1918 Gide became increasingly estranged from his wife, who died in 1938. In 1923 he fathered an illegitimate daughter whom he later adopted. During the occupation of France in the 1940s, Gide went into exile in Tunisia and then Algeria, returning to France in 1946. He was awarded the Nobel Prize for literature in 1947, and died of pulmonary congestion on 19 February 1951.

1

Nanima
24 September 1911

My dear Gide,

I exaggerate when I say that our correspondence is not regular; you have, I am sure, better excuses than I do to explain our long silence. We have found each other again, let us not lose touch.

My wife and I have returned to our life in the bush which, after all, is just as varied as Parisian life, but of another variety. We continue to watch over the things that grow—grass, cereals, wool and meat; they grow more or less, they die less or more, but there's nothing to complain about. And in the evening, after a hot bath that washes away the dust and the tiredness, we read in an English armchair, solid, deep and comfortable.

My reading? My dear fellow, you will be shocked at my intellectual nourishment. You will tell me that it is a hotchpotch, a Bombay curry bad for the digestion. Some Bret Harte, some Tristan Bernard,[1] some Shakespeare and some Léon Frapié![2]

I am still toiling away at the translation of Jack London's Love of Life; it's slow, but I'm counting on having the book finished at the end of year. By the way, tell me (1) if I can send you the manuscripts—(2) if you think you can find a publisher for L'Amour de la Vie.

146

L'Illustration should be publishing the first story in the book any day now; if you read it, you will be able to form an idea of the rest of the translation. If I am asking too much of you, just tell me to go away: don't feel embarrassed.

I am taking the liberty of sending two photos so as to keep us in your memory. The first one shows Hettie standing behind the sixteen ploughshares (3 ploughs) pulled by the steam tractor. We're not too 'stone age' at Nanima! The second photo shows Alexandroff—an eleven-month-old Borzoi, and his master that he loves, aged . . . that's nobody's business.

Just as I write this, on the verandah, Hettie is bottle-feeding a young fox found last week in a burrow full of rabbits. Hettie is really amazing with animals; I think she could bring up a young plesiosaurus if one was brought to her that had fallen out of the nest.

I have written once or twice to our friends the Laurenses;[3] but I suppose that a pen is heavier than a brush. At the earliest opportunity, remember us to them and tell Pierre that I am still waiting for his illustrations.

Hettie joins me in sending Mme Gide and yourself our best and most sincere good wishes.

Yours,
Paul Wenz

PS How is your work going? I am sending away for your latest book.[4] I enclose with this letter an issue of *Lilley's Magazine*— a new one which I fear will not live to a ripe old age. You will find yourself in singular company! Anyway, your fame has at last reached the Antipodes . . .

2

Nanima
31 December 1911

My dear Gide,

Thanks for your kind letter of 1 November. To begin at the beginning, I will explain the photo of the steam plough by saying that the machine pulls three ploughs, two with 6 ploughshares each and one with $4-12 + 4 = 16$. It is true that in the photo I can only see fifteen—the sixteenth is hidden. Don't count them again, just take my word.

About Jack London—I'm grateful that you are so kind as to concern yourself with my translation. I like to think that you will be able to read my manuscripts. So if your opinion and that of M. Roz are favourable, I'll let you do the rest, type it up at my expense if necessary, find a publisher, etc.

If you like the translation, I'll go so far as to ask you to do a little preface, not to present the translator, who is usually of no interest to the public, but to present Jack London. I think I have sent you his autobiography which he himself sent to me, and I could send you a photo or two of him if you think it would be useful.

Jack London translated into pretty, well-dressed French would, I think, be a mistake; on the other hand, it is possible that my own French has too many hobnails on its thick boots. I have tried to stay as close to the text as possible; you will be able to tell me sincerely how well I have pulled it off.

I am sending you by the same mail one half of the translation of *Love of Life*; the other half will follow next week.

I am just reading *Nouveaux Prétextes* which is not in the least boring (your word). I have learned from it so far, and I would love to read your critiques of contemporary writers! Last week I finished *L'Armature* by Hervieu:[5] I am no critic but my humble opinion is that it is Stupid with a capital S. Ditto for *Bruges la Morte*. In that case again, I am probably old-fashioned, or I didn't understand; but *Bruges la Morte* makes me think of a cherry pip mounted on a brooch surrounded with little diamonds. I like Bazin[6] in *Le Blé qui lève*.

Please send me your new novel and put your mark on it.[7]

I am trying to write something longer in scope, but I think I will only manage to get away from the short story with difficulty.[8] I am not giving up yet, but it's long in taking shape.

Tonight, 31st December, Hettie and I are installed on the verandah in a sort of giant meat-safe which protects us from

148

the mosquitos. The night is hot, the crickets and the frogs are creaking like badly oiled doors and sound like a boiler under pressure. They will go on doing that until tomorrow morning: that's their affair and it doesn't bother us. Shortly, before going to bed, we will sacrifice a bottle of champagne to wish a happy new year to all the family and friends over there on the other side of the salt water.

My wife joins me in sending Mme Gide and yourself our best wishes. Remember us to the Laurenses—remember me too to your young nephew and to M. and Mme Roz.

Yours,
Paul Wenz

3

Nanima
26 April 1912

My dear friend,

Thanks for your letter from Florence acknowledging receipt of the manuscript of the Jack London translation. I hope that the package was complete, I sent it in two parts.

As far as I can remember, I didn't send the autobiography of J.L., but asked you whether it would be useful. In any case— here it is, enclosed. He sent it to me himself, so it's authentic.

We are sorry to learn that the fair country of France is sometimes an unbearable hornets' nest; let's hope that the others will wear themselves out before you do. Here it's the drought, the Australian affliction which reminds us loudly that we have the responsibility for thousands of lives which, even if they are not human, no doubt have as much value as our own. Happily, my conscience is at rest on this point, I have enough to feed my animals, and I am even feeding (for payment) the animals of others.

Lawson has written a marvellous thing on this subject. There are some men trying to pull out of the mud some poor bogged cattle, too weak to get out by themselves. The clergyman comes

149

up and says: 'Brothers, let us pray to God that he might give us some rain, perhaps He will hear our prayers.'

One of the men replies to the parson: 'If God can't hear the cries of these poor beasts dying of hunger and thirst, He won't hear our prayers.'

L'Amour de la Vie has appeared in *L'Illustration*—illustrated by Devambez—I suppose it's the best Devambez could do, after all, you couldn't ask him to go to the Klondyke.

We've just got back from Sydney, where we had the good fortune to meet Amundsen, back from the South Pole. He's a charming man; I believe these Norwegians are the *cream* of the white race, they are still doing the few great things that remain to be done, they are handsome fellows with the fine souls of Vikings.

My wife joins me in sending to Mme Gide and yourself our best wishes. Remember us to mutual friends.

Yours sincerely,
Paul Wenz

PS Last week I had lunch on board the *Zélée*, in Sydney, with Commander W. Fischbacher from the Ecole Alsacienne. We hadn't seen each other for thirty years. Fischbacher thought I had grown taller.

4

Nanima
16 November 1912

My dear Gide,

The Auteuil to Nanima service inaugurated nearly two years ago is not working too well—and this letter is not going to restore it, on the contrary. My wife and I are planning to be in Europe next spring. Our intention is to leave Australia in February to go via Cape Horn to Montevideo—then Buenos Aires, Chili, Peru, Bolivia, the Amazon or Panama. All that is just pencilled in, but we'll know shortly whether or not we can reserve our cabin.

Right now we're well into summer, and, I will add, well into

150

the flies; for no man goes outdoors without having his face wrapped in a veil. Everything is starting to go yellow, except the lucerne, and scarcely a month ago, all was green and the garden was a riot of roses.

A club of bohemians called the 'Casuals'[9] invited me to dine one night in Sydney, promising me interesting companions and vile food. The cuisine was passable and the companions very amusing. A painter, two illustrators, two magazine editors, a parliamentary librarian. All more or less socialists, not too rich. The librarian, a small, ugly, comical Irishman, knows all that is being written in France;[10] he had read all of Gide except the *Nouveaux Prétextes*, which I sent to him. He is familiar with Charles-Louis Philippe, and he lent me *Bubu de Montparnasse*.[11] That evening was something very refreshing for me; we stayed together until midnight and nobody mentioned horses or football. You have no idea what that means in Australia! An Australian who doesn't talk about sport is almost as rare as a strainer without holes.

I can scarcely ask you what you are doing for I won't have your reply inside six months—I can only hope that Mme Gide and yourself are well and that life is weighing lightly on you. If you see the Laurenses, give them our best and tell them *not* to write now.

I toil away now and then—on Sundays especially—at a misshapen thing, ill-groomed and nameless: with time and patience it will perhaps make a novel.[12] One thing frightens me: I keep wondering if my French doesn't smell terribly of eucalyptus or mint or both!

Jack London, back from his New York–San Francisco voyage via the Horn on a sailing boat, writes to me this week asking news of *Love of Life* in translation. I think J.L. has given of his best in it, the first stories about Alaska and the Yukon are the best in the collection.

I have begun to read O. Henry's *Intentions*—an American humorist who died recently, quite young. There are some very good things in it.

My wife joins me in sending Mme Gide and yourself the best of our good wishes.

Yours sincerely,
Paul Wenz

5

Rheims
28 June 1913

My dear Gide,

Here we are once more disembarked from countries that are exotic, hot and dirty, but so interesting. The city of Cherbourg was all decked in flags when we set foot on native soil; but they told us that it was for M Poincaré[13] and not for us.

We took 102 days from Sydney to Paris; but we saw Cape Horn, Montevideo, Buenos Aires, Chili, Bolivia, Peru, Panama, Trinidad and Barbados. We crossed Lake Titicaca—at 3812 metres altitude—we saw lakes of borax, a lake of asphalt; in short, we got our money's worth.

I hope that you are all well and that we will be able to see you some day or other. As soon as you can, write me a note here and give us your news. Our best wishes to Mme Gide and yourself as well as to the Laurenses.

Sincerely,
Paul Wenz

PS Can something be done with the Jack London translation?

6

HOTEL SCHUTZENHOF UND RHENANIA
BAD EMS
1 August 1913

My dear Gide,

Thanks for your card dated from Tivoli (another country that I don't know). I intend to stay in France about a year—I should say in Europe, for we will also be going to England.

I have written to Roz; but he is too busy or too much on

152

holidays to reply by return mail—I don't blame him—above all I understand him.

We are leading a patriarchal life here; we are taking the waters by inhalations, garglings, baths, sippings. The respectable German wife is everywhere we look, we understand now why woman is of the neuter gender in German—she is certainly 'a thing' in skirts.

We are here for two or three weeks more.

Our best wishes to Mme Gide and yourself.

Sincerely,
Paul Wenz

7

Bad Ems
(Germany)
1 September 1913

My dear Gide,

I received yesterday a letter from Roz. He has read the London translation, seems very satisfied with it and tells me that it should be fairly easy to find a publisher. Do you think that the *Nouvelle Revue Française* would accept *L'Amour de la Vie*? I hope to be back in France in a week's time: send me your answer in Rheims.

Best wishes

Sincerely,
Paul Wenz

8

HOTEL SCHUTZENHOF UND RHENANIA
BAD EMS

6 September 1913

My dear Gide,

Thanks for your letter and thanks also for the trouble you are taking about my translation of J. London. I am going to write to Roz to send the MS to the *Nouvelle Revue*. Cure at Ems? *Ja wohl!* but slight results this time; I am coughing in German, that's all.

We hope to be in Rheims next Monday, there I'll be looking up Jo Krug who is my childhood friend, regimental comrade, brother-in-law of my brother; in short my fourth brother. Certainly, if we go to Bénouville and if Cuverville is not too far from there—we have a horror of distances—we will come to see you.

Our good wishes to Mme Gide and yourself.

Sincerely,
Paul Wenz

9

9 Knightsbridge
Hyde Park Corner
19 March 1916

My dear friend,

Thanks to the two letters of introduction that you were so kind as to give me, I have communicated with Conrad and Bennett. The former replied to me with an invitation to go and see him at home, the second gave me a rendezvous at his club, where I had the good fortune and the pleasure of taking tea with him. A. Bennett has been thoroughly charming with me; the way in which he welcomed me says a lot about the esteem and the friendship he has for you. He loves our country a great deal, he even says that he couldn't express how much he admires it.

Conrad's letter was full of kindness, and it will be a pleasure to go and see him one day, between a Saturday and a Monday.

I have written to Roz where you advised me to do so; I have heard nothing since about the manuscripts.[14]

My new functions as Delegate to London of the Under Secretariat of the Health Service (my friends are requested never to address me by this title) transform me into what I have never wished to be in my life, a man behind a desk. But this war is doing us some good, in that it is forcing us to accept all sorts of sacrifices.

My wife is making up parcels for soldiers out of articles sent from Australia to London; everything is of the best quality, and is accompanied by notes saying 'From your friends in Australia'

154

or even by letters from little Australian girls to little French girls. Verdun led to the Red Cross in London receiving a *flood* of cheques which has lasted for more than a week now. Up till now it has certainly been a moral victory, at least.

My wife joins me in sending you as well as Mme Gide our best wishes.

Paul Wenz

10

9 Knightsbridge
Hyde Park Corner
9 November 1916

My dear Gide,

It will no doubt interest you to know that I signed yesterday a Mission Order for J. Galsworthy and his wife who are going off to France to help our boys. He is going as a masseur to the Benevolent Hospital at Dié (Drôme).

I have given him your address in Rue Madame—for I know that he would like to see you. He will only be about two days in Paris—probably at the Hotel Regina—I think that he and his wife are leaving tonight for Paris, where they will only arrive tomorrow night, providing the service is not interrupted.

No news of Conrad for several weeks.

During my short stay in Paris, I went to the *Revue* where I was told that you were still in the country. I had more luck with Roz whom I went to see one Sunday morning: despite the time and the day he received me with his usual kindness.

The *Revue de Paris* told me some time ago that it would take more Australian stuff—if there was any. I am working as hard as I can on a bushman who has crossed the seas to come and 'take a bashing' with the other boys—and who finds himself disembarked in London.[15]

My wife joins me in sending Mme Gide and yourself our best wishes.

Yours sincerely,
Paul Wenz

155

11

London, 9 Knightsbridge, S.W.
30 July 1917

My dear Gide,

This letter begins with some????: How are you? What are you doing? Where are you?

Roz, whom I saw last May, didn't seem to have any very clear idea of your movements.

My wife and I are here, stuck for the duration of the war; quietly doing our humble and not very glorious task: she makes up bundles for the boys or serves in a canteen for Australians; I keep on signing Mission Orders for people who are going to France to help our armies or our hospitals.

We live in a small flat in St Johns Wood, a quiet spot, near Regents Park and the Zoo.

We often see the Australians; one of the men from my station stopped me the other day just as I was coming out of the office; the barriers fell, my stockman turned soldier came to dine with us the next day, after which I took him to the theatre with a fat cigar in his mouth. St Dunstan's where the War Blind are cared for, rehabilitated . . . and spoiled, is two minutes away from our house; we are regular visitors to the establishment, and I rarely miss going to see them dance on Friday evenings. The blind Australians also come to dine often with us, and we are glad to do something for them.

This contact with the Australians, blind or otherwise, suggested to me *Le Pays de leurs pères* which the *Revue de Paris* has, I think, accepted and which I hope will appear in a few months.

Roz has been to me a godfather of kindness and patience; but in spite of the hope he himself seemed to have, he hasn't been able to place either the childhood memories or the stories.[16] For a moment I had the illusion that the *Mercure*[17] would accept the memoirs; but nothing came of it. Anyway Roz is hanging on to my manuscripts, I hope they won't moulder away completely!

No news of Conrad; he doesn't see many people, and despite my desire to see him again, I didn't want to go and bother him without an invitation from him. Now and then I see Morley Roberts[18] who has written some very good things, among others *Time and Mr Waring*, a book that he would like to have translated into French. If you had the time to read it, I would send it to you.

Give us some of your news in your next letter, and please accept, with Mme Gide, from my wife and me our best compliments.

Yours sincerely as ever,
Paul Wenz

12

London, 9 Knightsbridge SW
15th November 1917

My dear friend,

No reply from you to my letter of 14 September. Did you receive it, along with Lancaster's book?[19]

I must write shortly to Jack London's widow; I will ask you to get the *Nouvelle Revue Française* to let me know what's happening with the sales of *L'Amour de la Vie*. Since the work appeared, I have received no sales account, I know absolutely nothing about its fate. I undertook with Jack London to give him half of my translator's royalties: I must therefore let his widow know what the situation is.

I very much regret that our friend Roz, despite his patience with me and the trouble he has taken, has not been able to place the 'memories of youth'; your opinion and his had made me hope that the manuscript might have found a welcome in one of the Revues.

I had occasion recently to see Davray several times, he is very busy just now launching the Anglo-French Society, which apparently is floating quite well and sailing under a fair wind. Ed Gosse gave us a very fine lecture a fortnight ago about the intellectual relations between England and France.

A play by Barrie, *Dear Brutus*, is having a lot of success, and it deserves to, for it is quite charming and amusing; one can find in it touches of Shakespeare, of Maeterlinck and . . . of Barrie.

I am now alone in London, my wife is in Cannes, working in the South African Ambulance; while occupying herself usefully, she is living in a climate that suits her better than the London winter.

I hope to hear from you soon: remember me to Mme Gide,

Yours sincerely,
Paul Wenz

13

9 Rue Dufétel
Le Chesnay
10 May 1919

My dear friend,

Your letter has just now reached me; I have just returned from Morocco, I am leaving this morning for Rheims and on Monday for London. I will see about your trunk of books and will do my best—so that you will get it in Paris.

I plan to be back here on the 16th or 17th of the month.

Our best wishes to Mme Gide and yourself.

Sincerely as ever,
Paul Wenz

14

Nanima
14 June 1932

Dear friend,

The Call of the Country has made itself heard, we have taken passage on the *Otranto* which is to disembark us towards the end of July at Toulon, a pretty seaport. We are going to make Versailles our headquarters to begin with; beyond that, our plans are vague and stretch indulgently between Copenhagen and Aswan.

We continue to enjoy the relative peace of the bush; moreover Nanima is coming to be a sort of Zoological Garden. The (wild?)

cattle scarcely bother to give way to us, the horses come and eat sugar out of our hands, the grey parrots get mixed up with the hens and the ibis eat grasshoppers fifty yards from the dining room. Australia is nevertheless going through a bad period of being broke and we all seem to be working (those who are working) for the love of mankind. The elections last Saturday have fortunately swept out quite a few vermin; but the cleaning up will last a long time.

F. Roz tells me that paper and ink have a lot of trouble selling; and the last MS that I sent him is I think still in the shop-windows.[20] Things are bad all over the world; good will towards men seems to have disappeared, and we feel we belong to a generation which has less fear of quitting this world, so gloomy are the prospects on this side of the divide.

In my last letter—for which you owe me a reply, I was telling you about Barrie's play *Shall We Join the Ladies*, and I hope that you haven't completely dropped the idea. If the play has not been translated, see what you can do through Maurois[21] to get Barrie's authorisation.

My wife joins me in sending Mme Gide and yourself our best wishes.

Sincerely,
Paul Wenz

15

Nanima
12 December 1933

My dear friend,

The preparations for our hurried departure for the Antipodes forced us to neglect many things and to leave France without saying goodbye—in English: 'to take French leave'!

Following your advice, I have chopped into the thicket of my MS—made the corrections indicated by you, except for 'fastidieux' which I forgot to change, and left the folder with Gallimard's secretary.[22] No news since the end of September.

We have got back into our bush existence as into an old

pair of slippers; we are amazed ourselves at our degree of adaptability. Our handsome Alsatian dog welcomed us with joy; *a week before* our arrival, he had become impossible: he had seen the preparations that they were making for us at the house.

I don't know if I have lost my judgement, but I often find myself alone in my opinion when it's a matter of giving an opinion on a book. For example *La Jument Verte*,[23] which I had begun on board the ship, leapt over the ship's rail at page 63—and that in sight of the Cocos Islands—I couldn't go on. In spite of all that, the book seems to be a success.

Our fond memories to Mme Gide and yourself, and to both of you our best wishes for 1934.

Sincerely,
Paul Wenz

PS Have found two English words for which we don't have a word in French: 'shallow' = *peu profond* and 'uncanny' = ?

I

Cuverville en Caux
16 June 1919

My dear friend,

I am torn between the dread of imposing on you and the fear that, if I do not mention once again that box of books, I may give you cause to say to me: you ought to have reminded me . . . Where is it? Have you been able to do anything to make sure that it was not lost on your last trip to London? In your last letter of May 10th you were telling me that as soon as you were in England you would worry about it and make sure that the aforesaid box was well and truly sent.

Has it disappeared? In that case, is there anything to be done? If it is lost, I would prefer that it should not be because of our negligence; therefore pray excuse me if I bore you a little by mentioning it again.

I greatly regretted not being able to come and see you again

160

(both of you) at that dinner with the Paul Laurenses. Kindly remember me to Mrs Paul Wenz.

Very affectionately yours,
André Gide

II

15 September 1932

M. Paul Wenz
My dear friend,

I am just back from Paris where I spent only a little time, but enough nevertheless to devote myself to a thorough search through the abundant purgatory of manuscripts which had been entrusted to me. Alas! no sign of your translation of Baring.[1] Being quite certain that I haven't destroyed it, I wonder (but in vain) to whom I could have given it; most likely, mistrusting my own judgement, I wanted to have someone else read it, but who?? I keep trying to remember and can't believe I didn't note it down. But I implore you, I repeat once more: before putting yourself to the task give the English text to somebody competent who can tell you whether Baring's text is worth the trouble and if there is some chance in the long run of seeing it accepted in France by a theatre company, a literary journal or a publishing house. Why not write directly to Maurois himself? No-one could be more helpful or obliging; you could, if need be, mention my name, as I am on the best of terms with him; I can even write to him if you wish, but I am still convinced that he would receive you just as well if you write to him yourself, although you may mention, in the course of conversation, that it was I who advised you to contact him.

Affectionately yours,
André Gide

III

Mr Paul Wenz
6 Boulevard de Glatigny
Versailles
Seine et Oise

14 September 1933

Dear friend,

This morning I received, at the same time, your letter and your manuscript, which I shall read immediately. I wrote to you yesterday, but without having your exact address; I hope that my letter, addressed simply to Boulevard de Glatigny, without indicating any number, may nevertheless get to you.

No, do not be unjust to Berl, the director of *Marianne*. You must believe that, on returning from his travels, he probably found a huge pile of urgent work, and not that he was 'trying to prolong his holiday'; but I will be going back to Paris in a few days and will have a word with him, as well as with Gallimard and Hirsch, about Jack London—as I have already done, I was telling you in my letter, with Malraux.

Yours,
André Gide

IV

Cuverville
Criquetot l'Esneval—tel: 27
Seine Inférieure
16 September 1933

My dear Wenz,

Excuse this bad typing: I have a slight touch of the shakes and it amuses me to type. Last night I finished reading your book[2], without skipping over a single line; happy to wander about with you all over the world. This technique of Whitmanesque sampling is far from displeasing to me; it lends itself to lyricism and becomes fairly heady sometimes; but sometimes as well one might wish for a little more selection, for all the fruits in your basket are far from being equally succulent; some are even quite

162

insipid. It would be easy for you to eliminate them. Last, but not least (and here I am putting myself in the shoes of the French reader), I fear that this constant humour might seem a bit monotonous. Some errors or infelicities of expression lead me to think that many of the sentences have first been thought in English (am I mistaken?): *'On danse souvent, et comme les 14 dames ont le choix de 60 danseurs, elles ne craignent pas de faire tapisserie'* ['There is often dancing, and since the 14 ladies have a choice of 60 partners, they are not afraid of being wallflowers']. No! *'ne pas craindre de'* ['are not afraid of'] expresses exactly the opposite of what you mean. You should say *'n'ont pas à craindre de'* ['run no risk of'].—*'le diamant me sert à couper sur les vitres que je coupe moi-même, une ligne droite qui est bien rarement respectée'* ['I use the diamond to trace on the window-panes, which I cut myself, a straight line which is very rarely respected']; no doubt you mean: a line which tries in vain to remain straight; but the words betray your idea.—*'extrêmement fastidieux dans le choix des oeufs'* ['extremely fastidious in choosing eggs']; that's the English 'fastidious', but the word *'fastidieux'* has never had that sense in our language, and can only mean 'wearisome, tedious'. One can also feel that it has not all been written at the same time, and some passages are a little dated: the little wooden stools given out by the usherettes in Paris theatres; and, if I am not mistaken, your description of the Panama Canal.—In your chapter on children: 'They have forgotten their Dickens, and the bit where David Copperfield . . .' Shouldn't it rather be Nicholas Nickleby?

Now it is my turn to tell you a little story. Some six years ago, I spent an execrable night in Hammamet, in a small hotel (the only one there was then). The pillow on my bed seemed to be full of foreign bodies completely incompatible with a Christian sleep. The next morning, I carried out an autopsy to get to the bottom of it, and I discovered in the said pillow, amongst the feathers of various birds, some chickens' heads and feet. An overzealous servant had emptied the whole lot, pell-mell, into the pillowcase.

I happened to relate the preceding tale to the Duchess of Trevisa, whom I had met in the Congo, who was then travelling in that country, and who had been commissioned by the magazine *Vogue* to write an article about her travels. The story was printed. It read: 'If you go to Hammamet, don't stay at the Hotel X if you don't like finding chickens' heads and feet in your pillow'; or something like that. The Hotel X immediately issued a writ for defamation, and won its case (cases of this sort are always won in France): the damages were 20,000 francs which *Vogue* had to pay to the said hotel (it had demanded 40,000).

Let this be a warning to you. Be careful! For the Turbian Funicular Company, for example, would be within its rights to demand 100,000 francs from you for having said that its traction system had some teeth missing.

Next time I am passing through Paris, I will take your book to the *NRF*, but with no great hopes, I must confess. In any case I will ask them to make a prompt decision about you so that you will be able to submit your text elsewhere in case they reject it. And will you give me permission to say that, if necessary, you would make a few cuts?

A thousand kind thoughts from my wife for the two of you.

Very affectionately yours,
André Gide

NOTES

[1] Tristan Bernard (1866-1947) was a very popular comic novelist and dramatist.

[2] Léon Frapié (1863-1949) wrote novels (about social problems) that were widely read at the turn of the century.

[3] Paul Albert Laurens was a post-impressionist painter who was a mutual friend of both Gide and Wenz; he painted a portrait of Paul Wenz.

[4] Wenz is probably referring to *Nouveaux Prétextes* (1911), a book of literary essays by Gide (see next letter).

[5] Paul Hervieu (1857-1915), author of the books mentioned, was a moralist writer popular with the middle classes.

[6] René Bazin (1853-1932) was a well known novelist at the turn of the century; *Le Blé qui lève* is a novel of rural life published in 1907.

[7] Wenz is probably referring to Gide's short novel *Isabelle* published in 1911.

[8] This probably refers to an early draft of *L'Homme du soleil couchant*.

⁹ The Casuals were a group of Sydney artists and writers which included figures such as Christopher Brennan and Jack Lindsay.

¹⁰ The 'librarian' mentioned by Wenz is most probably Christopher Brennan, who worked at the NSW Public Library before his appointment to Sydney University and who was well versed in French literature.

¹¹ Charles-Louis Philippe (1874–1909), author of *Bubu de Montparnasse* (1901) was a social realist writer and member of the founding group of the *Nouvelle Revue Française*.

¹² Wenz is probably referring once again to an early version of *L'Homme du soleil couchant*.

¹³ Raymond Poincaré was President of the French Republic from 1913 to 1920.

¹⁴ The manuscripts referred to are possibly those of *Il était une fois un gosse* and/or the war stories: see letter 11.

¹⁵ Wenz is referring to *Le Pays de leurs pères*, first published in the *Revue de Paris* in 1918.

¹⁶ Another reference to *Il était une fois un gosse* and, most probably, the war stories.

¹⁷ The reference is to the *Mercure de France,* one of the leading Paris periodicals.

¹⁸ Morley Roberts was a British writer of adventure stories who visited Australia a number of times and occasionally used Australian settings in his work.

¹⁹ Possibly refers to 'G.B. Lancaster', pseudonym of Edith Lyttleton, a Tasmanian-born writer and friend of Miles Franklin.

²⁰ The reference is to *L'Echarde*, published in 1931.

²¹ André Maurois (1885–1967), well known novelist, biographer and essayist, was also an enthusiast and an intermediary for English literature in France.

²² Wenz is referring to his unpublished manuscript *En époussetant la mappemonde*; in a letter dated 16 September 1933 Gide had sent some detailed criticisms and suggestions. Gallimard rejected the manuscript on 21 December 1933.

²³ *La Jument Verte* (1933) by Marcel Aymé (1902–1967) is a bawdy caricature of life in a French village.

¹ 'Baring' is probably an error for 'Barrie' (ie J.M. Barrie)—see Wenz's letter of 14 June 1932.

² The reference is to Wenz's unpublished manuscript *En Epoussetant la mappemonde* [Dusting Off the Globe].

AUSTRALIAN
CORRESPONDENCE

1

Nanima
7 August 1920

A. G. Stephens Esq.
Sydney

Dear Sir,
Many thanks for your kind criticism of *Le Pays de leurs Pères*
which I hope you read without too much effort. I am glad to
say such men as Marcel Prévost, Pierre Mille, Brieux and A.
Gide gave me much encouragement and spoke well of the book.
On the other hand, some NZ paper gave me a very poor show.
I am sure the man could not read French.
I am sending you 2 small books which were printed by the
'Instruction Publique' for some schools.[1] They are just small
sketches written in Reims during the bombardment and in London.
Just tell me the ones you like best.

Yours sincerely,
Paul Wenz

2

22 Manning Street
Potts Point
Sydney
13 May 1931

Dear Mr Wenz,
You have been long waiting for a signed copy of my poems.
I believe I even went so far as to promise you one as a gift.
I wish I could give you one, but alack! my small earnings

have felt the general pinch and I am reduced to hawking my wares.

Here is the tariff:

(a) signed copy: one guinea

(b) signed copy with owner's name written in, and corrections (two letters misprinted and two verses omitted by oversight in copy sent to press): one guinea & a half.

(c) same as (b) but containing an autographed unpublished poem (a different one in each, which limits the number of copies saleable, as there are very few *inédits* in such a state—at present—as to satisfy the author): two guineas.

So much for business.

I have been re-reading *Mme Bovary*: a lot of reflexions occur. I will chew them over and send them to you. After that *L'éducation sentimentale*.

Yours as ever (ie dilatory and apologetic)
Chris Brennan

3

6 June 1931

Read *L'écharde* in one sitting last night. Send me a note so that I know what you want me to do—article, notice, review . . .

C. J. Brennan
22 Manning St
Potts Point

(Original letter in French)

4

26 Grey St, Carlton NSW
7 June 1937

Dear Monsieur and Madame,

I have been trying to get a book for you entitled *Back to Bool Bool*, which I consider goes more beneath the surface than the general run of Australian novels, but cannot yet find a copy. It is one of the few Australian stories that I put on the shelf with *Such Is Life*. You will perhaps have seen my article in the *Bulletin* of May 26. Mr Palmer did not merely abridge this, our one great novel, he altered the text in a heinous manner in my opinion.

P. R. Stephensen has amusingly mentioned the author of *Back to Bool Bool* in the June *Publicist* and I send a copy.

I have not yet read *Dig* nor *Le Jardin des Coraux* as I have been so rushed. Had to do 10,000 words of biographical sketch in two days—one for research and the other for drafting, as Mr Clune informed me that Mrs Clune and I were going to roll down the Murrumbidgee with him. Both Mrs Clune and I tried to postpone this with the result that we both go at the screech of dawn tomorrow—a veritable abduction.

So I shall write at a later date in less haste and for the moment wish you to know what a real and rare delight was the visit with you both in your lovely home on that beautiful day.

Cordially,
Miles Franklin

5

13 July 1937

Dear Miss Franklin,

It was very nice of you to send us the book, and we thank you very much. I started to read *Back to Bool Bool*, and so far find much in it that lacks in many Australian novels. Of course, I had heard about the book many times: does anybody know who the author is?

Your visit and Mr Clune's are still remembered here, and we hope that now you know what they are like, you will come again—but not just for lunch! I think we could talk about a lot of things that have nothing to do with cows, wheat nor shearing. Hoping you had a nice trip, my wife joins me in very kind regards to you and Mr Clune.

Yours sincerely,
Paul Wenz

6

10 August 1937

Miss Franklin,

Your intimate knowledge of Australian life and your power to describe its atmosphere prompt me to ask you whether you might consent, should the occasion arise, to translate one of my books. It is unnecessary to add that I would leave it up to you to decide whether or not the book is worth the trouble. I do not know on what terms translations are done here; the translation that I did of *Love of Life* by Jack London has a contract signed on a fifty-fifty basis. In any case, I would be happy to submit to you a few chapters of the manuscript and to have from you an absolutely sincere opinion.

I have finished *Back to Bool Bool* that you were so kind as to send me. I liked the book, though it was a bit involved; but the characters in it are well defined and the plot is firmly filled out with drama and feeling.

My wife joins me in sending you our best regards.

Yours sincerely,
Paul Wenz

(Original letter in French)

7

Carlton NSW
14 July (a great French day)[2]
1937

Cher Monsieur,

Two evenings since I had an hour of repose—my first since I saw you—and took out *Le Jardin des Coraux*. I have not spoken a word of your language since 1918 nor read one for 12 years, and so found I had forgotten all my French, which never was, or was in the style of that mentioned on p122 in *Le Jardin*, and of which you must have met so disappointingly much in your life here.

However, with the aid of a limited and ancient dictionary, I was soon re-enchanted. I was alert to the way you have captured the sunlight, the colouring, the devotion to the *plage*, the uncomplicated physical life of the Australians without a deeper thought or worry—like a big, bright, wholesome but unfurnished room.

Then came yesterday your pleasing suggestion.[3] A congenial adventure, but alas, my days are tied. My people were prime examples of those Australians who lacked thrift and I am helpless—impaled upon dull and ceaseless chores.

Also, for translation one must know a language bi-lingually. I could not give you a sound opinion on anything in French. In regard to French I am merely an infatuate not a scholar. I revel in French for its difference and precision. The French way of looking at things makes me chuckle and gurgle but in proper translation all that would go.

(Just think of the difference between *All That Swagger* and *Le Jardin des Coraux*—in the tufts and linings as you would put it.)

But I have been thinking of something else—bigger—which would bring other translations in its train.

I meant to tell Madame how I treasured her that she had added you to Australia—a phenomenon and an enrichment—instead of permitting you to subtract her from us and taking her to France with its tilth of centuries of cultural accumulation and its cosmopolitan Paris.

This is what seizes me. You are not only a Frenchman who has entered into Australian life and affairs, but that much rarer animal, a Frenchman here who is a writer too. You are articulate. Why not do your life here, your early emotions, your experienced thought—that would be grand—a dodo of difference. Then here is the original idea, rewrite it in English for us. I could help you there: this would be the way to preserve those French turns of thought and speech which delight me, and surely would delight others of my national mentality and language.

I could do that translation with verve. It would be a transposition really. This seems to me to be a beguiling prospect, like the lantern under the boy's coat—to be kept secret and doted on till it grows and comes forth as a brave surprise. Put it in your head and heart and see if it grows.

I thank you very much for the compliment you have paid me in this invitation to translate. I am sorry that my opinion on anything French might be misleading. You must be lonelier than I am myself—solitary I mean—in the need of someone to whom you can submit your work for discussion. But I know many in the cities who do so much submitting and intertrading of flattery that they become mere Tantony pigs and the scars of isolation are not so bad as that.

Salutations to you and Madame from
Miles Franklin

8

26 Grey St Carlton NSW
18 September 1937

Cher Monsieur,

I am long in replying to your kind note but at present I am night and day nurse and it takes all my strength. I have had today to refuse the request to give a course of eight lectures on Australian literature in a University Extension Course. This is a subject near to my heart, but I am too worn out.

I have recently finished reading again your '*l'Homme au soleil couchant*' You are seized as I am with the vastness of the oblivion behind the first ploughing of this continent. I wanted to quote paragraphs but have lent the book to a friend who reads French and translates in the hope that it might result in a pleasant contact for you if nothing more.

Since have come '*L'Echarde*' and '*Diary of a Newchum*'. The first I shall read carefully as soon as I have a moment. The second I have devoured in half an hour. You too see the vast torture of animals here. The diary is a fine morsel. Your clarity and conciseness are exceptional and your observation lively and delicate. No, it is not a joke, but a valuable and intensely interesting piece of observation, very true to Australia and through a new pair of eyes. Gently and kindly done too. It is crisp and clear

171

English. Did you translate it? H. H. Champion of the Booklover's Library was a very dear friend of mine and I always stay with the family when I go to Melbourne.

Lucienne Mechin has married a young man of Tumut with 2500 acres and so we need not worry her at present. She will be absorbed in absorbing her new state and her new continent. May she be happily absorbed by both.

There is a strange history behind that Arab translation.[4] If you really knew me you would be more puzzled by finding it in my library. I have never read more than a story or two. That lush orientalism revolts me but it is necessary to be informed of other minds than those of one's own nation. Please do not destroy the volume. I mean to refer to it in a big novel which I have roughed out.

I am so weary please forgive this stupid letter. It was so kind of you to come out here to see me.

Kind greeting to you and Madame from
Miles Franklin

9

Nanima
Forbes
24 September 1937

Dear Miss Franklin,

I am sorry to hear that you have such a worrying time nursing, and hope that your patient will soon be better. I have finished *My Brilliant Career* and find it puzzling to get the 'real' out of the imaginative—so naturally and vividly it is written—I shall return the book when I come to Sydney, together with the 2 other ones—all safe in my keeping.

I am pleased to hear you liked the *New Chum*. I know I spoiled it by stringing through it the girl's story. At the time, I was weak enough to take D. H. Souter's advice.

Shall I bore you by giving you a rough résumé of the book

I have just finished? The title *Walkaringa* is the name of the small town I am describing—the hero a kid—description of Dad's farm—the Bush School—The finding of a Diprotodon skeleton on the farm—which means £200 to Dad—A Rush round Walkaringa—the kid has 'salted' a hole with 2 specimens of gold he stole from the School museum—The harvest, done for the widow—in one day—by 9 machines and 72 horses. The kid with a mate is now rabbit-trapping—One hot day, the very day the governor of NSW visits Walkaringa, the 2 trappers take their rabbits to the Railway. The inspector refuses them as they are getting less 'fresh' every minute. On their way back with their noisome (is that the word?) cargo—the horses take fright and the trappers' carrion finds itself hemmed in the procession—between the Band and the Governor's carriage. The hankerchiefs of the crowd cease waving as the rabbits pass. Visit of the Governor to the show station of the district—handsome home full of trophies—nothing else—champion rams and ewes. The atmosphere reeks of yokel—and the handsome place is as empty as a skull of everything beautiful to the eye or the brain. On the way back—the Governor stops at a bark hut where an old man lives—they say he is cracked—he shows the Gov. his books—both recite Omar K. and make friends over a pannican [sic] of tea.

Later, a letter for Jimmy—the hero—he is heir to a place in the Lake District in England. On board—to *his* estate—53 acres, 40 sheep and a nice mansion. But rain and dull weather, strange humour, drink etc—make him lonely. Snow—he loves it but catches a bad cold—Pneumonia—off to Nice to recuperate—then back home to Walkaringa—just tell me sincerely how it stands on its legs—Mary, his school mate knows on his return that his lungs are touched—but there is good hope of his recovery.

'I'll wait—Jim'—that is the end.

Yours sincerely,
Paul Wenz

Carlton NSW
28 September 1937

Cher Monsieur,

Your outline contains ideas for a very jolly story with amusing and human situations. It depends for the remainder on that blowing of the wind where it listeth and how much of that *le bon Dieu* permits us to list, so to speak.

Are you going to be in town before Oct 21? I mentioned you to G. B. Lancaster the other day (Edith Lyttleton) and she said she would so much like to meet you and Mrs Wenz again. If you could let me know in advance I thought it would be a pleasant surprise for her to have us meet for a cup of tea in town.

Excuse frantic haste,

Sincerely,
Miles Franklin

11

Nanima
Forbes
2 October 1937

Chere Miss Franklin,

Thanks for your letter and for your opinion about the outline of my MSS. I shall try to be in town before the 21st and we must arrange to have tea with Miss Lyttleton. I will let you know as soon as I decide to come down.

Hoping your patient is better—

Yours sincerely,
Paul Wenz

12

Carlton
Monday afternoon
18 October 1937

Dear Mr Wenz,

Mr Farmer Whyte rang up this afternoon to arrange to meet Miss Lyttleton and me tomorrow. I know that Miss Lyttleton is so full of engagements that it would be difficult to fit another in so I took the liberty of suggesting that Mr Whyte should come too. He is the editor of the *National Australian Review* and parliamentary correspondent from Canberra to the *Herald*, and a most kindly and interesting man. He is delighted at the opportunity of meeting you so I hope that this arrangement will meet your inclination, dear Monsieur, as I was not able to consult you beforehand.

Till tomorrow at the Australia

Sincerely,
Miles Franklin

NOTES

[1] The reference is to *Choses d'hier* (1918) and *Bonnes Gens de la Grande Guerre* (1919).

[2] Since this letter is clearly a reply to the previous one, this date is most probably an error for 14 August.

[3] See letter from Paul Wenz, dated 10 August 1937, above.

[4] Apparently a reference to Cheikh Nefzaoui, *Le Livre d'amour de l'Orient: le jardin parfumé* (Paris, 1912) which was part of Miles Franklin's library.

BIOGRAPHICAL OUTLINE

1834
17 May: birth of Emile Wenz, into a Protestant family from Wurtemburg; he will become the father of Paul Wenz.

1839
29 July: birth of Marie Dertinger, who will become Mme Emile Wenz and the mother of Paul.

1858
Emile Wenz, who has done his business apprenticeship in London, settles in Rheims.

1859
He founds the Etablissements Wenz, which will open agencies in Argentina, Chile, and Uruguay, as well as in Australia (in Sydney, Melbourne and Perth). During the 1914–18 war, they will transfer their address to Paris, 1 rue de Metz, in the 10th arrondissement. Their operations will continue until 1981.
29 September: marriage of Emile Wenz and Marie Dertinger.

1863
26 May: birth of Emile Wenz the younger. He too will be a wool-merchant, but also a pioneer of kite-borne aerial photography.

1865
Birth of Frédéric, who will become a painter and friend of Toulouse-Lautrec. Among other works, he will decorate the John E. Meritt house in St Louis, Missouri.

1869

28 January: birth in Adelaide, South Australia, of Harriet Adela Annette Dunne, future wife of Paul Wenz.
18 August: at 9 pm, birth of Paul Wenz in Rheims.

1872

Birth of Alfred, who will go into the family business, like Emile.

1873

Birth of Aline, the little sister, who will become Mme Courtois.

1875–77

Paul goes to school, to 'the asylum', with the Sisters of the Infant Jesus.

1876

4 December: Major William West receives Nanima from the Crown, in exchange for the payment of £40 5s.

1877–79

Paul goes to grammar school in Rheims.

1879–88

Paul is a student at the Ecole Alsacienne, for part of the time in company with André Gide, whose friend he will remain. He lives in Sainte-Beuve's old house, transformed into a school dormitory, at 11 rue du Montparnasse, in the 6th arrondissement. He fails the *baccalauréat* at his first try.

1888–89

Paul does his military service in the 13th Artillery Regiment at Vincennes, where he meets up again with his best friend, Joseph Krug.

1889–90
From Monday 25 November 1889 to Saturday 19 February 1890, Paul is in charge of the Petty Cash desk at the Etablissements Wenz and feels cooped up in his grilled cage.

1890
Paul spends eight months in England.

1891–92
He spends thirteen months in Algeria. The climate doesn't suit him, among other incompatibilities.

On 21 January 1891, Nanima becomes the property of Sarah Saul West (unmarried sister of the deceased major) and her brother William Perry West.

1892
On the *Rimutaka*, Paul makes his first trip to Australia, from Tilbury to Hobart via the Cape in forty-one days.

On 20 October, Paul and Joseph Krug meet again in Ballarat, the gold city.

1892–1894
Paul spends time as a jackeroo on sheep stations in Victoria and New South Wales.

1894
He takes the *Rimutaka* again to return to France, via the Strait of Magellan and Montevideo.

1895
Paul seems to have stayed only a little time in France, for in January, he is in New Caledonia.

On 5 August, he is in Mackay in Queensland, where he is looking for the wreck of a rather hypothetical boat that is supposed to have brought over some survivors from the La Pérouse shipwreck.

1896

He sails once more for France. On the way over, probably, he passes through Paraguay: in any case, he is there on 23 July. He meets William Lane, the founder of the utopian New Australia colony.

On the boat bringing him back to Australia, he meets his future wife.

1897

He is already living at Nanima, the magnificent station on the banks of the Lachlan, midway between Forbes and Cowra in New South Wales, 400 kilometres west of Sydney. He is getting ready to buy it and is probably staying in the cottage, dating from around 1890 and still in existence.

His brother Alfred comes to visit him.

1898

2 April: J.F. Rowe, builder, is contracted to build a residence at 'Nanama Station' [sic] for the sum of £1,133 10s by the architect J. Bates.

13 April: Paul signs the title deed for Nanima conjointly with William Percy Dobson, grazier.

15 September: he marries Harriet Adela Annette Dunne, daughter of a grazier from the Darling region. She has three sisters: Sahalie (the future Mrs Plunkett), Mabel and Lilian (the future Mrs MacLennan).

1899

5 January: Paul, in Sydney, in the presence of A.J. MacDonald, solicitor, and Edward J. Beeby, clerk, dictates and signs the will in which he leaves all his property to his wife. He will never make any other.

1900

6 October: Wenz's first two stories to be published appear in *L'Illustration* under the pen-name 'Paul Warrego': '*Comment Bill*

Larkins alla à l'Exposition' ('How Bill Larkins Went to the Paris Exhibition') and '*Fred, Scène d'Australie*' ('Fred, an Australian Story').

1902

February 4: Paul Wenz becomes the sole proprietor of Nanima, a station of 5000 acres.

1904–1905(?)

What Paul calls their 'honeymoon' takes him, in company with his wife, from Sydney to Saint-Nazaire, via Manila, Hong Kong, Japan, the USA, Mexico and Havana. They must have left in 1904, probably on the *Derflinger*.

In any case, on 28 July 1905, Paul is in Rheims, for on that date Joseph Krug lends him 100,000 francs, for a period of five years at 4% interest.

And that year, Paul Wenz publishes his first book: *A l'autre bout du monde* [At the Other End of the World]. Sub-titled 'Australian adventures and manners', this collection of sixteen short stories bears the name of 'Paul Warrego' as the author and 'La Librairie Universelle' in Paris as the publisher.

Why this pseudonym? It is borrowed from the name of a river, lying mostly in Queensland, which Paul most probably knew quite well. A psychoanalyst would no doubt notice that the Warrego flows into the Darling; he would see in it echoes of the young husband's unconscious. Without going that far, the same initial W and the Australian flavour suffice as an explanation. Let us move on to a too hasty listing: '*Le Vagabond*' [The Swaggie] fits straight into the tradition of tales of the bush: a swagman stumbles by chance onto the traces of a former gold-seeker, like himself, who once robbed him of all his nuggets and has since become a prosperous farmer, married, and a family man. But you cannot guess the ending.

'*L'Evadé*' [The Escapee] introduces us to the crew of a lighthouse, on the coast of Queensland, reduced to four people among whom suddenly appears an escaped political prisoner from the penal

180

colony in Noumea.

'*La Sécheressé*' [The Drought] tells how a woodcutter who wanted to become a gold-seeker turns into a squatter and runs into forces stronger than himself.

'*Jim et Jack*' [Jim and Jack] is reproduced here.

'*Une soirée à Tonga*' [An Evening in Tonga] belongs to the genre of reportage. It is the literary expression of an unusual real experience.

'*Fausse alerte*' [False Alert], on the other hand, probably owes much to the author's imagination (even though, with Paul Wenz, one often wonders when he tells a story whether it is not perhaps a true story that has been reported to him!). Following a tragic mistake, due to drink, on a sailing ship laden with copra, the captain throws four bodies into the sea. He has killed his sailors, and he commits suicide. When the authorities finally discover his corpse alone on his own vessel, they blame the natives of San Cristobal: 'Shortly afterwards, a warship went to the scene of the murder; a few dozen black natives were killed, a few villages burned; civilisation felt itself satisfied, for the brave captain was avenged.'

'*En Nouvelle-Calédonié*' [In New Caledonia] is also the story of vengeance, but a real and more justified one. It tells of the revenge that a Tonkinese, employed by the manager of a nickel mine, perpetrates upon a French officer who, not long before, had executed several of his compatriots.

'*Charley*' will be found in the present volume, together with '*Picky*' and '*Comment Bill Larkins alla à l'Exposition*, [How Bill Larkins went to the Paris Exhibition].

In all justice, we should summarise the other six stories, but this sketch already reveals what links Paul Wenz to the master writers that he greatly admired: Joseph Conrad, Rudyard Kipling, Jack London. Authentic and profound, his own experience will fill out and animate his way of telling stories soberly, without affectation or exaggeration, using the appropriate word and giving the exact detail.

The book will have a second edition in 1907.

1906

21 June: The famous critic A.G. Stephens reviews *A l'autre bout du monde* in the *Bulletin*.

1908

What was the date of his return? The end of 1905? Nanima, which was also his creation—a magnificent work—is now developing, under his driving energy and that of his wife. Under the pseudonym once more of 'Paul Warrego', a book is published in Melbourne, at the Book Lovers' Library in Collins Street. *Diary of a New Chum* is an exception: the only work in English by Paul Wenz. This diary of an immigrant fresh off the boat is a collection of impressions and anecdotes which are broadly autobiographical but in which invention and the taste for fiction also have their part. It is republished here for the first time since the 1920s.

1909

Having sailed to Australia in September 1908 on their yacht, the *Snark*, Jack and Charmian London develop a friendship with the 'Wenzies', as they call them. Howevever, they are unable to come down to Nanima (see Wenz's account in this volume, here published in translation for the first time).

Aboard the *Van Spilbergen*, Paul and Hettie Wenz arrive in Hong Kong, via Surabaya and other island ports.

On 19 May they are in Peking. Then they take the Trans-Siberian Railway.

From 22 to 29 August, Paul attends the first international aviation meeting which takes place in Rheims. He serves as an interpreter, especially for Hiram Maxim (an American famous for the machine-gun which bears his name). He also attends the banquet given in Paris in honour of Blériot.

While in France, Wenz visits André Gide and renews his old friendship.

182

1910

The Wenzes have returned from Europe with their nephew Jean (son of Emile Wenz) who accompanies them to Nanima, where they arrive on 1 June.

Jean Wenz has left a diary (unpublished) of his stay at Nanima. This is the year of *Contes australiens* [Australian Stories] published by Plon, for the first time under the name of Paul Wenz. In 1910, the title was to have been *Sous la Croix du Sud* [Beneath the Southern Cross], but from the second edition in 1911 this title is relegated below the other one. In the list of his works, Paul will subsequently stick with *Contes australiens*.

'*Le Cockatoo*' [The Cocky] is set in the district of Forbes, where Nanima is situated (it is fairly rare that Wenz is so explicit; normally he transposes and recreates his own space, as also his own time, which, in the long run, is that of his youth). The cocky is a small farmer who has obtained a poor quality run from the Crown; he steals sheep from a wealthier neighbour who has just acquired the property. The thief's daughter is pretty, but the ending is unexpected.

'*Tallicolo*' recounts the misadventures of a missionary in a small Pacific island. Quinine plays a large part in the propagation of his faith, but an unchecked epidemic of measles has nasty consequences for him.

Seven other stories follow, including '*Son Chien*' [His Dog] and '*55 minutes de retard*' [55 Minutes Late], together with '*La hutte des becs-cuillers*' [The Spoonbill Hut] and '*Le Charretier*' [The Waggoner], all of which will be found in this volume. '*Le Charretier*' first appeared in the *Nouvelle Revue Française* number 15 of 1 March 1910, and it was not at all unworthy of its surroundings.

1911

24 September: Wenz writes to Gide that he is well advanced on the translation of Jack London's *Love of Life*. On 31 December he sends the completed manuscript to Gide and Firmin Roz. In the accompanying letter to Gide, Wenz mentions that he is

working on the first draft of a novel (no doubt an early version of *L'Homme du soleil couchant*, see below).

1912

April: Wenz meets Roald Amundsen in Sydney after his return from the South Pole. On the 26th he writes to Gide to recommend Henry Lawson to him.

16 November: in another letter to Gide, he mentions his travel plans for the coming year and says he is 'still struggling with a shapeless thing that might turn into a novel'—he also worries that his French 'might be starting to smell of eucalyptus.'

1913

1 March: Paul leases some of the land at Nanima until 29 November 1926 to James Dick Hill, a grazier from Yass (about 130 km from Cowra and 60 km from Canberra).

28 June: the Wenzes arrive in Rheims after travelling via Cape Horn to Buenos Aires, then across to Chile, Peru and Bolivia and on to Europe via the Panama Canal, Trinidad and Barbados.

1914

Love of Life by Jack London is translated by Paul Wenz and appears as *L'Amour de la Vie*. Having become a friend of Jack London in 1909, Wenz brought him to the attention of André Gide. In 1912 the latter consulted Jean Schlumberger about Wenz's translation *L'Amour de la Vie:* although he 'didn't like it much', he did think that London was going to be 'in vogue'. Auguste Anglès says: 'Wenz's translation was buried' (see *André Gide et le premier groupe de la NRF*, vol 3, Gallimard, Paris, 1987, p 160).

On returning to Paris in September 1913, Wenz took up the cause again. He won through, and the first edition by Gallimard bears the date 1914.

Paul Wenz's translation is still currently available in the paperback collection '10-18 (V.G.E.)', but Firmin Roz's preface has not been reprinted. This future member of the Institut, quite familiar with the English-speaking world, was, with the critic Henri Ghéon, favourably inclined from the beginning to Wenz's writing.

1914-18
The war catches Wenz and his wife just before their planned return from France. Wenz is mobilised and attached to the Franco-British military hospital service. During the hostilities, he will cross the Channel fifty-three times.
From March 1916 he is posted to London, with the French Committee of the Red Cross.

1915
April-May: serial publication of *L'Homme du soleil couchant* in the *Revue de Paris.*

1916
March: Wenz, now posted to London, meets Joseph Conrad and Arnold Bennett.
9 November: in a letter to Gide, Wenz mentions that he has begun work on his second novel, *Le Pays de leurs Pères* (see below).

1917
30 July: in a letter to Gide, Wenz speaks of frequent contacts with wounded Australian soldiers in London; he has sent the completed ms of *Le Pays de leurs Pères* to the *Revue de Paris*, and he also mentions other mss that he has sent to Roz (probably *Il était une fois un gosse* and the war stories).

1918
October-November: serial publication of *Le Pays de leurs Pères* in the *Revue de Paris.*

1919
January: Paul and Hettie are on the Côte d'Azur.
April: Wenz accompanies the Australian Mission to Morocco as liaison officer and interpreter.

In this year, Wenz publishes with Berger-Levrault two small collections of war stories, which was natural in the circumstances. His own style, half documentary, half fictional, can be found once more in them. He has observed, he has been moved and he tells about it. He does it well, but, of course, unlike when he tells about Australia he is not the only one to do so.

Bonnes gens de la Grande Guerre [Ordinary People in the Great War] is a collection of six stories, one of which is about an Australian soldier on leave in London. Seven other stories are collected in *Choses d'hier* [Things of Yesterday].

A first-rate work in which we find him in full possession of his talent is a novel of 250 pages published the same year by Calmann-Lévy entitled *Le Pays de leurs Pères* [Land of Their Fathers]. The plot is simple: a slow, discreet love story about a young Australian soldier, who has been blinded, and his English nurse. There's nothing original in that, any more than there is in a colourful episode in which an aging aristocrat is reunited with the grandson he had never seen. What counts and carries away the reader is the authenticity of the characters, both principal and secondary, and the wealth of realistic detail. It is the understated and lively tone of the story, shot through with cordial humour. It is the Australian light which shines through on every page.

Dedicated 'to the men who came from Australia and New Zealand to fight for France—to the memory of those who stayed behind in the soil of France', this novel is as non-conformist as it can be because of its true subject: the Australian character. Of course the key is a standard one, but the gate opens onto a garden such as had not been seen before in French novels.

In November the Wenzes return to Australia.

1921
December: Wenz notes 'Have re-read *Madame Bovary*'.

186

1922

12 March: the celebrated soprano Nellie Melba receives the Wenzes at her home at Coombe Cottage near Lilydale (about forty kilometres from Melbourne).

1923

L'Homme du soleil couchant [The Sundowner] is published, once again by Calmann-Lévy, after having been serialised in the *Revue de Paris* in 1915. It is a novel of 220 pages which was announced as being 'soon to appear' as early as 1919, but it was in fact begun before the Wenzes left for Europe prior to the 1914-18 war.

It is dedicated 'to an Australian who has made me know and love Australia, my wife.'

The 'sundowner', or swagman, is the man who turns up right on sunset, too late to work, but just early enough so that he cannot be refused a meal. He has probably known better days . . . For love, Harry Preston has set sail for Australia, leaving England behind. A man of means in the first chapter, when he has no other cares than those of a passenger in love, he finds himself in the second chapter in Sydney, ruined and alone. It is in the Royal Hotel in an isolated township called by the fair name of Pallamallawa that he begins to get his confidence back, having now become the bar pianist.

He gets himself three mates, knowingly described by Wenz. They will cause a town to spring up around a gold deposit. And there will be an unexpected reunion between Harry and the woman he loved, in the setting of a brand new school . . . The love story once more counts for rather little beside the re-creation of an atmosphere, the resuscitation of an era—that of the 1890s. The one when 'God save the Queen' was still sung in honour of Queen Victoria . . . that Paul Wenz knew so well in his youth! How well he knew what the birth of a school meant, since it was he who donated the land and the library for the school which was founded at Payten's Bridge, not far from Nanima.

1924

4 April: Hettie Wenz renews her French passport in Sydney. She has 'blue eyes', a 'straight nose', a 'natural complexion'. She is 1.56 metres tall (5'1½")—her husband was at least 1.96 metres tall (6'5"). Weight: he, 105 kilograms; she, less than 60 (in Ceylon in 1927).

In April, they sail on the *Makura*, which is headed for Vancouver via Suva.

6 May: they disembark at Cherbourg.

In May, they arrive at Versailles, 6 Boulevard de Glatigny, the home of Madame Courtois (née Aline Wenz), a widow since 6 April 1920.

On 9 August in Paris Mrs Wenz buys a book by Paul Le Chevallier, *Les oiseaux chanteurs*. (It can be found today with other books that belonged to the Wenzes, and which the Mitchell Library did not take, in a dusty cellar in the Forbes Literary Institute. To dust off, catalogue and display these books, some of which are valuable, alongside the portrait of Wenz by Paul Laurens, which is in the small museum at Forbes, as well as some photos taken by Wenz, is a project dear to the heart of all Wenzians.)

18 November: the Wenzes pass through Calais.

1925

In February they leave Europe once again.

29 April: after the Canary Islands, we find them in Dakar.

They travel to the interior of Senegal.

In July they go to Capetown and Durban.

In this year, Wenz publishes with the Librairie Larose *L'élevage du mouton en Australie* [Sheep-raising in Australia], with a preface by Henry Geoffroy-Saint-Hilaire, and four photos and eighteen illustrations by Frédéric Wenz. Unlike many authors who are all too willing to talk about something they know nothing about, Wenz has a thorough grasp of the subjects he discusses. His essay can be read with interest and pleasure. Some pages read like a short story, such as the account of the purchase of Nanima.

Paul Wenz has his own way of being personal without showing off.

1926
3 September: death of Emile Wenz, 'the founding father'.

1927
21 July: the Wenzes are in Georgetown, on the island of Penang in Malaya.
13 September: in Colombo.
October: they arrive in Marseilles, where Mme Courtois is waiting for them.

1928
The Wenzes are in France.
On 3 November, in The *Brisbane Courier*, Nettie Palmer, who with her husband Vance is already an important figure in Australian culture, devotes a favourable article to Wenz—who, writing in French, was not known in his adopted country. 'The author is no mere visitor [. . .] he knows this country as few French writers ever could. [. . .] He is no tourist, like Pierre Benoit, who was here last year.'
Pierre Benoit wrote *Erromango*, which is not without a certain charm mixed with a vague exoticism: reading it only brings out what makes Wenz's work solid, true and lasting by comparison. 'It's time these books of Paul Wenz appeared in English; at least, it is long past the time for most Australians who can read French to make their acquaintance!' adds Nettie Palmer.

1929
In March, the Wenzes, accompanied by Mme Courtois and her daughter Alice, are back in Sydney.
The *Bulletin* dated 13 March contains a new article by Nettie Palmer (on *Le Pays de leurs Pères*), and she meets Wenz for the first time at his hotel (most likely the Australia) that same week. She had written: 'Our Frenchman has been a good Australian,

too . . .' quoting with amusement words like *le swagman, la station, la creek, le store,* which Wenz was fond of using.

16 April: Paul Wenz writes to Alfred Wenz and Joseph Krug to recommend to them Mrs Jack London, who is coming to France. This same year, Calmann-Lévy publishes *Le Jardin des Coraux* [The Coral Garden]. The displacement of time, a sort of lack of temporal precision—that lack of concern or that perpetual tentativeness which characterises the work of Wenz—have never been so evident as they are here.

Although we can easily situate this writer in space (he is Australian in France, French in Australia—even if it is not such a comfortable situation, it is at least clear!), we have trouble situating him in time, since he was ahead of his own. Here is a novel as unlike the Parisian-style novel of the 1930s as possible. In fact it comes straight out of 1895, the year in which Wenz travelled on the Queensland coast, just before the prison colony in New Caledonia was closed (1897).

The Great Barrier Reef is the setting for the novel's action: an escaped convict from the Ile de Nou, landing miraculously on a small island where a young Sydney couple has chosen to spend their honeymoon, kills the husband and is killed by the wife. The rest is the story of an adolescence, or two adolescences, in Sydney—the details (the typically Wenzian little facts) of a modern Robinson Crusoe existence in the tropics. We will hear more of it.

1930

Il était une fois un gosse [There Was Once a Silly Kid] is published by the Editions de la Vraie France (Dunod), whose literary director is Firmin Roz. A book of amusing memoirs, sometimes transposed, sometimes direct, but always very discreet and perfectly simple. What are in fact short stories, such as 'L'Oncle d'Australie' [The Australian Uncle] or the story of the bookbinder who gets an inheritance, keep out all traces of egotism. The real letting down of the barriers, for Wenz, is already the act of writing. It is in the telling of stories that he told about himself. What did he

190

have to hide, anyway, that he should reveal himself in the way André Gide did? The sadness of not having any children when Hettie lost the one she was expecting? He gave birth to an Australian literature in French. And that is something that can be resurrected.

There are two confidences: Wenz admits, jokingly, to 'a thirst for fame'. He also says 'Very early on, I was certain that I was made to live far from cities.'

Paul Wenz justifies the publication of his memoirs by the fact that he has broken a leg and must stay in bed for a month. That is probably an author's invention, and letters to Gide seem to indicate that the manuscript had been written during the war and held by Firmin Roz since 1917.

1931

We have a few definite dates: on 27 April, 4 October and 16 December, Wenz writes from Nanima to Joseph Krug. On 13 May the poet Christopher Brennan (little known in his own time) writes to him from Sydney. On 6 June there is another letter, this time in French: 'Lu *L'Echarde* d'un trait, dans la soirée d'hier . . .' ('Read *L'Echarde* in one sitting last night . . .')

29 October: Mme Alphonse Daudet (born in 1847) writes to say she finds *L'Echarde* 'interesting for its details of exotic life, but the character of the emigrant woman, so obsessed, so exaggerated, makes the novel difficult to read and that's a pity, for it is written with care and is truly literary . . .' *L'Echarde* [The Thorn in the Flesh], a novel of 240 pages, was published by Firmin Roz at the Editions de la Vraie France; it was republished in 1986 by 'La Petite Maison', with a foreword by André Gide and an introduction by Jean-Paul Delamotte.

This is the only novel by Wenz that is currently available. It is the reverse of a love story set in South Australia in the early 1900s.

On 12 November in Melbourne, Nettie Palmer is visited by Wenz; he discusses literature with his usual discretion, but enthusiastically outlines his plan to use charcoal for running tractors.

1932

6 April: letter from Nanima to Joseph Krug.

9 June: the Wenzes sail from Sydney on the *Eridan*, bound for Marseilles.

July: Hettie and Paul are in Toulon, where they meet up with the Courtois family.

4 September: they begin a month's 'cure' at the Park Hotel in Bad Ems.

14 December: at the Villa Cynthia in Monaco, belonging to the Wenz family.

In this year, Anne Pearson Maryott, of 6357 Kimbark Avenue, Chicago, begins a translation of *L'Echarde* into English. Her manuscript has only recently been rediscovered.

1933

6 January: still at the Villa Cynthia.

February: the Wenzes travel in Provence. On the 11th they join the *Hilary* (Booth Line, Liverpool) in Lisbon, which sails on the 13th for Manaos, 1600 kilometres from the mouth of the Amazon. On 28 March they are back in Lisbon, and on the 29th they are in the Grand Hotel in Bayonne.

12 April: back in Monaco.

16 September: André Gide writes to Wenz at Boulevard de Glatigny with some detailed criticisms of the manuscript of *En époussetant la mappemonde* (cf below) which Wenz had sent him.

6 October: they sail from Toulon on the *Orford*. Paul Wenz will cross the equator for the fourteenth time. During the voyage he visits a fellow passenger, Rudyard Kipling, in his cabin.

13 October: serialisation of *Le Jardin des Coraux* begins in *Le Petit Marseillais.*

21 October: in Colombo, at the Grand Oriental Hotel.

21 December 1933: Gaston Gallimard rejects *En époussetant la mappemonde* (cf below).

1934

16 March: Marie de Saint-Exupéry writes to the Wenzes, who are at Nanima, to thank them: 'May God bless both of you for having helped me. Thanks to you, I have been able to set up a small workshop . . .' The letter refers to a book binding workshop for tuberculosis patients.

4 April: a story by Wenz appears in the Sydney *Bulletin*: 'The Most Beautiful Harbour in the World'.

9 August: from Paris, 28 rue Scheffer, the Comtesse de Bellefonds writes expressing interest in taking up the film rights for *Le Jardin des Coraux*: 'The more often I read your book, the more I tell myself that it is impossible that it should not be seen on the screen one day!'

Wenz has his books included in the Centenary Book Exhibition organised by the Australian Literature Society in Melbourne.

1935

12 June: Paul and Hettie are on West Molle Island in the Whitsunday Passage, North Queensland. They holiday there for three weeks.

24 June: they are in Sydney.

6 July: back at Nanima.

12 October: in a letter to Dr L.D. Woodward, a French lecturer at Sydney University, Wenz mentions that he has tried to interest a Sydney publisher in his work.

22 December: still at Nanima.

1936

28 January: Wenz writes from Nanima to Joseph Krug.

14 March: he writes to Krug from Wellington, New Zealand, en route to Rotorua.

23 April: from Sydney he writes to Alfred Wenz.

25 May and 12 June: letters from Nanima.

27 August: from Nanima he writes to Mme Jeanne Krug, Joseph's wife.

October: the Wenzes are in Sydney.

1937

May: Miles Franklin and Frank Clune visit the Wenzes at Nanima; Paul presents Miles Franklin with a copy of *Le Jardin des Coraux*.

13 July: Paul writes to Miles Franklin to thank her for sending him *Back to Bool Bool*.

10 August: Paul proposes that Miles Franklin translate one of his books; later in the month he visits her in Sydney and presents her with a copy of *L'Homme du soleil couchant*.

September: at Nanima; Paul is completing the manuscript of *Walkaringa*. He sends copies of *L'Echarde* and *Diary of a New Chum* to Miles Franklin.

18 September: Miles Franklin writes to express her enthusiasm for *L'Homme du soleil couchant* and *Diary of a New Chum*.

19 October: Paul has tea with Miles Franklin at the Australia Hotel and shows her the manuscript of *Walkaringa*.

29 October: letter from the Australia Hotel in Sydney to Joseph Krug to announce their next trip to Europe.

1938

In January (according to the letter to Joseph Krug), or more probably on 8 February, the Wenzes embark at Noumea on the *Eridan*, a ship of the Messageries Maritimes. Thence to the New Hebrides, Tahiti, Panama, Curaçao, Martinique, Guadeloupe and Madeira.

In March they arrive at Marseilles, to be met by Mme Courtois. They stay in Monaco.

In July Paul Wenz attends French–Australian memorial ceremonies at Villers-Bretonneux.

14 December: in Versailles, staying with Mme Courtois.

16 December: Firmin Roz writes that he has made approaches to Jean Fayard (*Candide*) and P. Gautier (*La Revue Bleue*) about publishing some texts by Wenz, in particular 'Le dernier film', 'Le Misogyne' (of which I have found no trace) and 'La Gazelle' which is included in the present volume.

1939

16 March: Bernard Barbey of the publishing house Fayard rejects *Walkaringa*.

17 March: Gaston Gallimard also rejects this manuscript: 'Our overloaded program does not permit us to devote to your book the launching and publicity which we feel is necessary for it to make its mark with the critics and the public . . .'

In March they embark at Toulon.

17 June: Paul Wenz returns from Melbourne to Nanima with 'a cold'. He receives some medical care, has a relapse and finally agrees to be hospitalised in the Crombie Hospital in Forbes.

19 August: a cable sent to Paris by the Wenz and Co office in Sydney announces that Paul Wenz is gravely ill.

On Wednesday 23 August at 7 am Paul Wenz dies.

On the 24th at 11.30 am he is buried in the Forbes cemetery.

On 28 August Fred W. Learoyd (Manager of Wenz and Co in Sydney) writes to Alfred Wenz: 'At the funeral there were a lot of people from the district, there were lots of flowers, and the pallbearers were all employees from Nanima.'

Comforting Mrs Wenz were one of her sisters, a niece, and her nephew, Norman Plunkett.

On 31 October at the reading of the will, his estate is valued at £40,664 6s. 8 d.

1948

Nanima is affected by the law granting land to returned soldiers.

1949

Mrs Hettie Wenz moves to the Hotel Pacific at Manly.

1959

Friday 22 May: death of Mrs Hettie Wenz. She is buried in the Forbes cemetery, in the same grave as her husband.

Nanima was sold, through the Perpetual Trustee Company, in 1960. It changed hands in 1963. Since 1975 it has belonged to Mr and Mrs John Bruce, and it is now run by their son John and their daughter-in-law Barbara. The property now consists of approximately 900 hectares. It has a flock of 3200 ewes. The house remains almost intact, except for tasteful modernisation, and is still just as simple and as beautiful.

In 1953, Professor L.A. Triebel of Hobart was preparing a biography of Paul Wenz. What has become of it? In 1969 *Le Courrier australien* marked the centenary of Paul Wenz's birth with articles by A.R. Chisolm and Erica C. Wolff (in the *Annuaire français d'Australie*, 1969–70). Another piece by Jeanine Miller also appeared in this publication. A radio play, *The Master of Nanima*, written by Marion Ord and produced by Peter Whitlock, has been broadcast by the ABC.

The Oxford Companion to Australian Literature (1985) has devoted a detailed article to Paul Wenz. Dr Maurice Blackman has prepared a biographical note to be published in the *Australian Dictionary of Biography* Volume XII (to appear in 1990).

In France, through various articles (*Le Monde*, 5 December 1982 and 14 June 1985, *Magazine littéraire*, April 1984, etc.) and the republication of *L'Echarde* in 1986 and *Un Australien Tout Neuf* [Diary of a New Chum] in 1989, the process of oblivion has been halted. The publication of this volume will, it is hoped, re-establish the name of Paul Wenz in Australia.

THE UNPUBLISHED MANUSCRIPTS IN THE MITCHELL LIBRARY

Apart from a superb album of photos taken by Wenz and a box of correspondence in which can be found some letters from Christopher Brennan, Miles Franklin and André Gide among others, the papers kept at the Mitchell Library in Sydney essentially consist of three unpublished manuscripts:

—A collection of twenty-eight short stories, including six tales for children '*L'Eléphant et la Tomate*', dedicated to Claude Gonin and dated 4 September 1933, was published in *La Semaine de Suzette* on 14 March 1935); five 'oriental' tales ('*L'Homme qui resta debout*' and '*Les Sandales*' appeared respectively in the Christmas issues of *L'Illustration* for 1935 and 1940); a short story written in Peking in May 1909 and another in Surabaya the same year; a New Zealand story and one Australian story, '*Joe le Solitaire*,' which is included here, along with '*La Gazelle*'. It is a manuscript of 215 pages.

—*Walkaringa,* sub-titled 'Scènes d'Australie' (287 pages), is a novel which goes right back to his beginnings, recreating a turn-of-the-century atmosphere and recounting the ties that linked (and still do, to a lesser degree) so many Australians to the 'Old Country'. The English part concerns us less than the properly Australian part, but the work is far from being negligible and there are plans to publish it at some stage.

—The third manuscript, *En époussetant la mappemonde* [Dusting Off the Globe] (276 pages), will be published soon through the Association Culturelle Franco-Australienne. This collection of memories and impressions from throughout the world, arranged in a sort of cinematic montage, effectively reveals the life and work of Paul Wenz in their full range and in a new light. An extract about Jack London is included in this volume.

It only remains to talk about the correspondence. So many letters have disappeared! How many notebooks? On 27 April 1931 Wenz wrote to Joseph Krug that he had rediscovered a detailed diary of their youthful wanderings around the coast of England. There were probably many others. Will they ever be discovered?

Jean-Paul Delamotte
and Maurice Blackman

ACKNOWLEDGEMENTS

The inspiration for this volume comes from Jean-Paul Delamotte, writer and translator and animating spirit of the Paris-based Association Culturelle Franco-Australienne. Monsieur Delamotte is also an enthusiastic champion of Australian letters in France and he has a particular interest in the work of Paul Wenz— 'that very strange animal, a French writer living in Australia', as Miles Franklin called him.

It is Monsieur Delamotte who organised and encouraged a group of Australian Wenz enthusiasts, including Frank Moorhouse, Margaret Whitlam, Patricia Brulant and myself, to collaborate in making sure that this selection of his writings will draw attention to a rather unique figure in Australian literature who has been all but forgotten since his death in 1939, and that it will perhaps lead to further translation and publication of his work in Australia, his adopted home.

The unpublished stories and memoirs of Paul Wenz are published with the authorisation of the Perpetual Trustee Company Ltd of Sydney, with the permission of the Mitchell Library of the State Library of New South Wales where typescripts of the stories are available, and with the assistance of M. and Mme Denis Wenz and of M. Claude Gonin in Paris. The letters of Paul Wenz to André Gide are reproduced in translation with the permission of Mme Catherine Gide and are published here for the first time. The other letters are published with the permission of the Mitchell Library.

Diary of a New Chum is republished here for the first time since the 1920s. Some of these texts were collected and published by Jean-Paul Delamotte in a special number of *Le Lérôt Rêveur*, number 46, December 1987; they are reproduced in translation by special arrangement with Jean-Paul Delamotte and the Association Culturelle Franco-Australienne.

Patricia Brulant's translation of 'Fifty-five Minutes Late' originally appeared in *Australian Short Stories* number 22, 1988, edited by Bruce Pascoe.

Maurice Blackman

OTHER TITLES IN THE IMPRINT SERIES

BUILDING ON SAND

David Parker

Building On Sand is a moving, often humorous evocation of the 1950s and 1960s in Adelaide. Subtly crafted to bring out the inarticulate tensions of childhood and adolescence in postwar Australia – a world of Aussie Rules, 'New Australians', souped-up Holdens and the first wave of rock and roll – *Building On Sand* was acclaimed by the critics and was shortlisted for the 1989 Miles Franklin Award.

'David Parker's first novel is a charming, affectionate reminiscence about an Adelaide childhood ... The prose is unaffected and straight-forward, the perspective always that of the young boy of the story seeing the world (and later himself) with the undeceived precision of childhood...Parker describes the elusive, fleeting mood exquisitely...'

Margaret McClusky, *The Sydney Morning Herald*

'The novel is an exercise in peeling back the layers of the mundane. Yet the subject matter – youth and growth – is always fascinating, and the tale is told in a quiet but strong, accomplished flow.'

Heather Falkner, *The Australian*

'It is a novel written with the skilful interplay of passion, assurance, subjectivity and detachment ... These events are firmly rooted in Parker's strong evocation of place in the novel...'

Amanda Lynch, *The Canberra Times*

THE PROGRESS OF MOONLIGHT

Barry Westburg

'I first became a private detective at the age of ten, but it was nearly a year before I cracked my first big case, the Dr Burpee Caper. Until then I had to contend with pigeonshit falling from the skies, the Italianate multiplication table and a premature potbelly.'

So begins the 'progress' of Sonny Thorwaldssen and his Uncle Moonlight down the Yellow Brick Road of Life — from the Midwest of the USA to Buzzard Swoop Ranch in the Wild West, and then below the equator to a fateful family reunion on a jetty in the Land of Oz. A saga of three generations of one eccentric family, Sonny's history takes us inside the space industry and the peace movement — as well as behind the walls of Sapsucker College for Spoilt, Rich and Incredibly Creative Women. Along the way we meet a rogue's gallery of wildly erratic and sometimes dangerous characters, including Go-Go Grannie (pistol packin' seventy-year-old disco dancer), Buckshot Rick (Tracer of Lost Persons, inventor of Thorglas, gaolbird), Love-and-Death-in-the-Afternoon Willie (drug-crazed bikie, fighter pilot), and the weird and lovable Uncle Moonlight himself, who was bumped on the head by a 1931 Chevy and has behaved oddly ever since.

'. . .a brilliant and very funny creation, full of noise and energy and boundless invention.'

Peter Goldsworthy

A MAN OF MARBLES

Rod Usher

Stavro ('Stan') Kristopolis is a greengrocer in Melbourne, working in the shop of his parents. They, and many of the customers, find it hard to categorise Stavro: he does things grown men don't do, yet places no demands on life. He is wide open in a world closed down by convention and conformity. He plays games. His particular game – the old sport of innocence, the gamble of goodness in a wicked world.

'Usher has quietly attempted some very difficult things in his novel, grounding motivation in mystery in an excessively explanatory age, creating a character of uncloying niceness and strong passivity.'

Les Murray, *The Age*

'For the all too rare achievement of presenting us with a book that can be read and savoured afterwards as well, Usher stands to be congratulated. And read again.'   George Papaellinas, *The Melbourne Herald*

'An unusual book from a talented writer who makes one wonder what his next venture will be.'   Peter Pierce, *The Sydney Morning Herald*

'Stavro is a permanently memorable creation...the novel's ending is as psychologically necessary as it is unexpected.'

R J Stove, *The Australian*